In Quest of the Pearl

In Quest of the Pearl

A NOVEL BY
SYD BANKS

Duval-Bibb Publishing Co.
Tampa

In Quest of the Pearl

Published by Duval-Bibb Publishing Co.

Copyright © 1989 by Syd Banks

All rights reserved.

Published in the United States by Duval-Bibb Publishing Co.

First Edition

Cover Photo: Syd Banks

Cover Design: Richard Mayer

Printed in the United States of America

First Duval-Bibb Publishing Co. edition: 1990

97 96 95 94 93 92 91 90   10 9 8 7 6 5 4 3 2 1

Library of Congress Cataloging-in-Publication Data

Banks, Syd R., 1931 -
    In quest of the pearl : a novel / by Syd Banks. -- 1st ed.
      p.   cm.
    ISBN 0-937713-02-3 : $10.95
    I. Title.
    PS3552. A494Q4   1990
    813' . 54--dc20   89-50502
                                             CIP

For additional copies or bulk orders, contact:

Duval-Bibb Publishing Co.
P.O. Box 23704
Tampa, Florida 33623 U.S.A.
(813) 870-1970

In Quest of the Pearl

This sequel to **Second Chance** is both captivating and fascinating, as it takes the reader on an intriguing journey that will never be forgotten. You are invited to step into a landscape of great beauty and powerful feelings, as you accompany one man returning to the island of Maui on his search for the "Pearl of Wisdom."

The original book, **Second Chance**, explains how Richard Sullivan had come to Hawai'i from New York, recently widowed and suffering from terminal cancer, when he was introduced to something which, inexplicably, resulted in the disappearance of his illness. He was given a glimpse into a deeper reality, which bewildered his intellect, but changed his life.

Now, he returns to Maui, to the two people who had shared with him their mystical knowledge, friendship, and Aloha:

Jonathan, a gentle prankster, who delights in showing you how, at times, you don't know what you think you do, tricking the reader into a deeper dimension of thought; and Mamma Lila, a beautiful, older Hawaiian lady, full of love, deep wisdom and compassion, whose enigmatic words hold the secret to the Wisdom of the Ages...for those who are ready to *Hear*.

This is a book that will captivate you, as you travel the island of Maui on an adventure beyond your wildest dreams.

For those who have ever wondered if there is more to life than meets the eye, this is the book for you.

In Quest
of the Pearl

<u>Chapter</u> <u>1</u>

Return to Maui

After I had been informed by my doctor that the cancerous cells had miraculously left my body, I felt such relief and happiness for the gift of health that I could hardly contain my emotions.

The following day I phoned Jonathan to tell him. He was overjoyed to hear everything had gone so well for me.

"By the way, would you please give my love to Mamma Lila, and tell her the good news?"

In Quest of the Pearl

"Certainly, it will be my pleasure," he said, "I know she will be happy to hear of your good fortune."

We said our goodbyes, and as I hung up the phone, I knew deep in my heart that someday I would return to Hawai'i.

About fourteen months later, the opportune time arrived when the company I work for shut down for a month to do some major repairs on the equipment. As soon as I heard of the closure, I was on the phone to my travel agent. In two short months I would leave New York and return to Hawai'i via Los Angeles.

In no time at all the two months passed by. A couple of good friends of mine, Tom and Barbara London, had volunteered to drive me to Kennedy Airport. Arriving on time, we had to make our way through hordes of travelers trying to find their airlines.

By the time I had waited in line and checked my baggage, the airport speakers were announcing that Flight 261 to Los Angeles was ready for boarding. Barbara, stepping forward to embrace me, wished me "Bon Voyage." Tom grasped my hand and said, "We wish you all the best. You be sure and have a great time." After a final embrace, I left them to board my flight.

The journey to Los Angeles passed swiftly as I

busied myself completing some unfinished paper work, and before I knew it we had crossed the continent to California.

There was a half hour wait for the change in crew and passengers before our departure for the Islands. It wasn't until a lovely Polynesian flight attendant appeared at my side to serve drinks that I truly realized I was on my way back to Maui.

Flying high above the Pacific, I couldn't help but think back on my last visit to Hawai'i. The beautiful scenes and magic moments I'd already spent there came flooding back to me again - from the singers at the lu'au on the island of Kaua'i, to the quiet beaches where I'd strolled in the morning, and the sunset by the seawall in old Lahaina where I first met Jonathan Davies. At first Jonathan had appeared as a man of about 50 years, medium height, slight build, with black hair and penetrating blue eyes. His soft voice had a rare quality of gentleness, and he gave the impression of being totally relaxed. However, as time went by, I learned there was far more to this man than there appeared to be. He was an exceptional person who spoke in such a mystical manner, that to this day I still haven't figured him out.

I had poured out my story of pain and

3

confusion to him and he had spoken to me about hope, and an answer to my dilemma. It had seemed impossible to me then, but somehow during the few weeks of my stay in Hawai'i, I discovered some part of that answer. *Something* had happened to me there that was both mystical and intriguing, and I desperately needed to find out what it was.

I felt an incredible sense of anticipation at meeting Jonathan again. I could only hope to see once more the beautiful and mysterious Hawaiian woman he had introduced me to. Mamma Lila was unlike anyone I had ever met. She was the most unique and loving individual I have ever encountered, a petite Hawaiian lady with thick beautiful grey hair, which she wore pulled back into a bun. Her age was very difficult to guess. She was one of those people who are often described as ageless, although by her history, my estimate would put her in her mid or late eighties. She, like Jonathan, had a mystical knowing, and a charismatic air about her that I had never seen in any other human being. She had told me of a reality deeper than the one I had known. In her wise and gentle way, she helped me to catch a brief glimpse of the inspiring vision she held of the world. I had heard and read many concepts, theories and philosophies about happiness and

4

the meaning of life, but Mamma Lila was the first person I had ever met who was actually filled with that happiness and peace of mind. Her every word, every smile, every breath, gave expression to that peace and happiness.

As I sat back in my seat I thought of the evening we had spent together, watching the glowing sunset as the trade winds drifted through the palms. I knew that I was returning to try and discover for myself the secret to the "pearl of wisdom" she had spoken of.

We flew over long, sloping beaches as we made our approach, and soon were taxiing towards the terminal. To my surprise, when I walked through gate 10, I saw a familiar old straw hat above the crowd. Sure enough, it was Jonathan.

He came toward me with a smile and shook my hand, greeting me warmly. "Aloha, Richard! Welcome back to Maui."

We walked together towards the baggage area. Jonathan's casual, friendly greeting made me feel as though I had never left the island. We walked back into each other's lives without any break in our friendship. One thought in my head couldn't wait to be answered. I asked Jonathan if he had seen Mamma Lila lately.

"As a matter of fact, I have. Only last night I had dinner with her. She's here in Lahaina

visiting some old friends of hers. I think you met them last time you were on Kaua'i; Mr. and Mrs. Makua."

"Yes, I'll never forget the picnic we had there. How long will Mamma Lila be staying here on Maui?"

"I'm not sure, but probably for a few weeks."

"I'd love to see her again."

Jonathan assured me that Mamma Lila was looking forward to meeting me again as well.

After we collected my luggage, we were on our way. I wanted to stay closer to Lahaina than I had the last time, so I had reserved a room at the Lahaina Shores Hotel. The drive from the airport took about forty-five minutes. After coming from a congested city like New York, the spaciousness that lay in front of me was overpowering as we drove past rolling fields of sugar cane stretching out to the sea. Also, I had forgotten the beauty of the West Maui Mountains; the way they fill the senses with their ever-changing soft pastel colors, bringing a feeling of tranquility. Jonathan drove slowly, also appreciating the beautiful scenery before us.

After a pleasant trip along the winding coastal highway, we turned off at a road marked by a sign that read "Front Street." The side of the road was bordered by all types of tropical foliage and

flowers. Almost hidden behind them were quaint little houses fronting the ocean.

Jonathan said the hotel was just down the road, and as I looked up I noticed a large flag floating lazily in the trade winds, atop a high, red tile roof. As the hotel came into view, I was surprised by the colonial plantation architecture. Many rows of white columns, capped by softly curving beams, were joined by several floors of white railings of the outside lanais.

We stopped under the rotunda of the hotel and walked into an old-fashioned lobby, open towards the beach. I noticed several small groups of people, some obviously families, enjoying their holidays by the pool. The hotel had a welcoming feeling about it and I was glad that a friend had recommended it.

A beautiful bouquet of anthuriums and other exotic flowers caught my eye as I approached the lovely young Hawaiian woman behind the reception desk, and introduced myself.

"Aloha, Mr. Sullivan," she said, "Welcome to the Lahaina Shores. We have your room waiting for you; I'm sure you'll like the view of the ocean."

While she completed the registration card for my room, I looked up for a moment towards the water as the sun dropped behind the neighboring island of Lana'i. I couldn't help thinking about

how it is said that the lure of the Islands intoxicates many visitors, making them believe the local saying "Maui no ka oi," (Maui is the best). At that moment there was no doubt in my mind - "Maui no ka oi."

<u>Chapter</u>
<u>2</u>

Beyond the Word

There is a belief in the Islands that it takes at least three days before newly arrived visitors settle in and see Hawai'i as it truly is. Perhaps it's true, for it wasn't until my fourth morning in Lahaina that I was feeling rested and ready to venture out from my hotel. After finishing my breakfast I drove over to Jonathan's, where I found him outside working in his yard.

His home was a small, old Hawaiian style

9

cottage with a tin roof. In the yard, as small as it was, he had banana, papaya and avocado trees, all laden with fruit.

"Would you care for a cup of coffee, or something cold to drink... iced tea?" Jonathan inquired.

"Sounds good, I'll try the iced tea."

After we had settled in, I told Jonathan how, in the past year, I'd thought a lot about him and Mamma Lila. Since my last visit to Hawai'i there had been many changes in my life. My outlook on life had altered dramatically.

Jonathan gave me a somewhat perplexed look. "Is your outlook on life better or worse?" he asked.

"Oh, much better. Of course, getting my health back changed my outlook, but it isn't just that. It's something much deeper. For example, I used to view my parents through a lot of hurtful memories; my feelings towards them were filled with resentment and confusing emotions. After my stay on Maui, I found myself describing them to someone as two beautiful, kind, loving and generous people. I had never consciously changed my mind about them, it just happened, and I honestly can't explain how or why!"

Jonathan bowed his head as if deep in thought. "If you just accept your good fortune and never

10

mind *why*, perhaps you will find the answer to that question on your OWN. But rest assured, when you *HEAR* the answer you are looking for, it will make a good account of itself; so much so that it will put to rest all your misinformed ideas and beliefs."

He told me that such knowledge would "break the boundaries of time" and "evolve my thought system" instantly, instead of my waiting for time to solve the mystery for me! Jonathan's statements never ceased to amaze me. I asked him to please explain what he meant in more depth.

With a stern look on his face, he said, "Again I tell you one must learn to *LISTEN*, and when this feat is accomplished, you will find the answers on your OWN. Believe it or not, the knowledge you are looking for is already within your own consciousness, waiting to be *realized.*"

I had forgotten that Jonathan often gave unusual answers, answers which at times didn't make too much sense. Since my last visit I had become more aware of the fact that his words couldn't be taken at face value. The last time I was in Hawai'i, Jonathan had me so confused with his mystifying statements that I just couldn't figure him out at all. However, once back in New York, a lot of what he'd said started to make

common sense.

The sun was like a ball of fire. There was very little breeze and I felt stifled. I mentioned my discomfort to Jonathan and he immediately suggested we take a drive "up country."

"It's a beautiful part of Maui, on the way up the slopes of Haleakala, which means 'House of the Sun.' It's a dormant volcano about 10,000 feet high, and I'm sure you will find it much cooler. The people of old Hawai'i regarded it as a special, sacred place."

As we drove along, I asked him what he thought of the psychic realm. I had heard about people who used crystals, tarot cards or other means to make connections with the world beyond the one we see. I was especially interested to hear Jonathan's views on psychics who could go into trances and convey messages from disembodied beings, or spiritualists who could communicate with ghosts.

Although Jonathan often displayed great patience, he didn't hesitate to let me know if he thought my question was inappropriate and irrelevant. Shaking his head from side to side, he said, "I realize there are many who believe in such rituals wholeheartedly. That is their privilege. But as far as I'm concerned, forget it!" A slight wave of his hand emphasized the words.

12

In Quest of the Pearl

"So you don't believe in ghosts?"

"Not one bit!" Jonathan answered.

"What do you think of mediums, then?"

Raising his old straw hat from his eyes, he glared at me, then he gave a big sigh. "Are you talking about mediums here on the island, or mediums in general?"

"Mediums in general," I replied.

An unusual seriousness I had never seen in Jonathan spread over his face and he said, "Oh! I see, that makes the question even more difficult!" He then gave me the following answer: "There are a great many mediums in this world; however, there are also many larges, not to mention a great percentage of smalls. But in general, I would say most people fit into the category of mediums!"

For a microscopic instant, I thought Jonathan must have misunderstood my question. Then I saw a little twinkle in his eyes, and burst out laughing as I caught the joke. I'd been had once again. Jonathan's laughter at my walking into his trap was so infectious I soon forgot all about mediums, ghosts, tarot cards, crystals, or anything else! I had received his message!

When our hilarity subsided, Jonathan spoke up again, "Actually, I remember walking through a local fairground and there was a booth where a woman was set up telling fortunes. She called

13

herself Madame Fifi, and for a dollar and a half she'd tell your future and assist you on your way to financial success. She must have been ignoring her own advice; the poor creature was shabbily dressed and drove the rustiest car I'd seen for a long while. To be honest with you Richard, my heart felt for her predicament in life. However, once I looked into a deeper reality, I realized that the situation this young woman was in was exactly what she wanted. It was *her* dream come true. Her freedom of thought was in action, and she was in the right place at the right time. Her fate had led her to whatever she thought or saw in life... just like you or anyone else!

"I find it a strange phenomenon that people accept superstitious mumbo-jumbo, such as bending spoons, communicating with ghosts, and a host of other irrelevant subjects as they travel on their journey to finding True Knowledge. I hope you don't think that I'm talking in a derogatory way. Believe me, I realize the innocence of self-inflicted thoughts, because we are all human."

Leaning over, Jonathan commented, "I would be going against my own philosophy if I denied the existence of the psychic realm. Neither could I deny that there are people who have special gifts in this field. All I am saying is look in the inner

realm and don't get caught in the trappings of the outer superstitions, where no answers lie. Be careful when you hunt for such knowledge. After all,

> 'A dog that barks up the wrong tree
> isn't much of a hunter.'"

The drive was as Jonathan had predicted, cool and pleasant. We stopped to gaze at the peaceful beauty that lay in front of us and I started to think again about the last time I had visited Maui. I remembered Jonathan saying that stress was detrimental to our well being and created disharmony in life.

At that time I'd failed to see his point of view, so I hadn't hesitated to express my feelings that a little stress never hurt anyone, and that I thought Jonathan wrong in his belief. I asked him if he remembered the conversation.

"Yes! I remember," he replied. "Why?"

I started to explain to him that the furniture company I work for is relatively small, with approximately thirty employees, and that it had always had a kind of family atmosphere. The company had been doing well, with output and profit last year surpassing our expectations.

"At least that's the way it was until my return to

New York last January."

"What happened last January?"

"It all happened on my first day back in the office when I was informed that the owners, in their infinite wisdom, had hired a management consulting group. This group had convinced them that since the company had made such good profits in a non-stressful situation, 'imagine what could be accomplished by creating some "motivational stress" to get the workers to be more productive.' Two weeks later all hell broke loose, as their main consultant began to threaten employees, telling them about the new 'up or out' policy which simply meant that they would be out the door looking for a new job if they didn't start producing more. It didn't take too long to realize that this highly aggressive behavior had disturbed a hornet's nest.

"Fights broke out amongst personnel. People started complaining about their jobs - jobs they'd been happy with for years. This type of behavior had been unknown in our company. I tried to reason with the consultant by explaining that his attitude was creating considerable discord throughout the operation, decreasing production rather than increasing it."

"What did he say to that?" inquired Jonathan.

"He said that if I didn't conform, *I* would be the

16

next to go! Well, to cut a long story short, within a month the balloon burst, when our best and most efficient tradesman was fired for laughing with his co-workers and appearing too carefree at his job. Apparently, our expert saw his cheerful attitude as a sign that he was not taking his work seriously enough. When I heard about it, I tried to get him to reverse his decision regarding Bert, the tradesman. I showed him Bert's impeccable record for the last fifteen years, proving that he had been the best producer, and had won the outstanding achievement award several years running.

"I kid you not, Jonathan. He looked at Bert's records as if they were non-existent. He got very upset and said brusquely, 'What would happen if everyone had Bert's happy go lucky attitude towards work? Nothing would be accomplished!'

"'But the records prove this same cheerful man produced more than anyone else!' I protested.

"'I don't care about *proof!*' yelled the expert. By this time he was obviously very annoyed and quite anxious; he had always been an intense person, but this time the intensity was almost overpowering. At that moment, for some strange reason, I thought of you, Jonathan, and then the most mystifying experience of my life took place. In the midst of this intense and strained

17

situation, the office seemed to *brighten*, as if it were filled with an energized force so strong I could feel it. His agitated voice, so loud a split second before, suddenly faded into the background, and the next thing I knew the man standing before me appeared to change in front of my eyes! I began to truly *see* that this unhappy, frustrated man *couldn't* hear my point of view. He was so lost in his preconceived ideas and theories that anything which didn't fit into his scheme of things he either ignored or considered wrong.

"Honestly, Jonathan, that was the most unusual, mysterious moment of my life. All of a sudden I felt compassion rising up like a wave within me, and I was truly sorry for the suffering this man was experiencing.

"This happened so quickly that a moment later - a blink of an eye really, yet it seemed timeless - things looked normal again, almost. The angry man still stood before me, the office regained its usual appearance, and the volume of his voice returned to normal. But something was definitely different, and I knew it was me. I slowly turned my gaze back to the consultant who was just finishing his tirade, when he turned on his heel and vanished through the door.

"Things continued along after that, and really, it

18

was like a nightmare. The whole plant was falling apart at the seams, and the owners were refusing to look at what was happening; until one day we lost our two best salesmen, who refused to work under such unnecessary, ridiculous stress. It all came to a sad end three days later, when the evening security guard found our consultant lying in a drunken heap in his office, ironically, a victim of stress."

For the longest time, Jonathan said nothing about my story. Finally, he asked how the consultant was doing. I told him that the man was still undergoing treatment for his alcohol problem, and that he was no longer with the company.

"Poor man," said Jonathan, "he must have gone through a lot of misery. I feel truly sorry for anyone addicted to alcohol. That old devil's brew can be undermining to both mind and body, but Life being a contact sport, there is no such thing as immunity from the trials and tribulations that it brings. There is no way that you or anyone else is going to escape from getting their bumps throughout life. However, the more wisdom you can find for yourself, the more you can learn to avoid the unnecessary bumps.

"It's like playing any other contact sport: a wise player avoids unnecessary injuries."

19

Thinking about my own life, and all the painful experiences I had gone through, I asked Jonathan, "How do you know what's avoidable and what isn't?"

"Find wisdom," he repeated. "Wisdom is the antibiotic of the soul. It is wisdom that clears the passages of the mind, bringing you the power to *SEE* and *HEAR* beyond the capabilities you now possess."

Pointing to his head, Jonathan started to explain to me that simplicity of *THOUGHT* is the guide to take me back to what I already know, but had forgotten due to a severe case of "congestionitis" of my thought system.

With his unusual sense of humor he then suggested I get some "noggin exlax," and that it might rid me of some of my impacted negative thoughts, better known in the medical field as "mental constipation."

I had to laugh at the image, and at Jonathan's knack of saying the most outrageous things, yet with a kindness behind his words that made it impossible to take offense. "You know, Jonathan, after that experience when I suddenly saw that man with a deeper understanding, my feelings of sorrow for him were so overwhelming, I couldn't help thinking how lucky I was not to be in his shoes. And to think, all I had done was listen to

the philosophy of two beautiful people and for some unknown reason, I was given a very special gift, a gift that grows each day, bringing positive feelings I had forgotten ever existed. I was like a little child again and the world became one gigantic academy of learning. I knew I had moved into another dimension of Thought:

>One of more positive feelings
>One of more understanding
>One of more gratefulness.

Does this make any sense to you Jonathan?"
"Yes, it makes perfect sense to me."
Reaching over, he laid his hand on my shoulder, his blue eyes sparkling like lights.
"My boy, I am proud of you."
Jonathan's words touched me deeply and I was filled with gratitude at having found a true friend.
The scenery was beautiful as we continued our drive. I was surprised to see large cactus growing along the sides of the road. Fat cattle grazed contentedly in the fields as gentle mists descended from the higher ground.

<u>Chapter</u> <u>3</u>

Form & Formlessness

The beautiful Maui days seemed to blend into each other, and one morning several days later, I half awoke from a deep sleep to find the sun pouring through a gap in the drapes of my hotel room. I lay drifting comfortably in that world midway between dreams and reality. It was a pleasure to realize that I had nothing planned for the day, no obligations or responsibilities. Gratefully, I relaxed into slumber once again.

23

In Quest of the Pearl

When I awoke a second time it was late morning. Opening the drapes, I was delighted by the sight of another spectacular day. The sun was shining brightly, and light trade winds ruffled the palm trees by the beach below.

Ever since my arrival on Maui I'd been looking forward to seeing Mamma Lila again. I dialed the number of the Makuas, where Jonathan had told me she was staying. When she came on the line I was surprised by the warmth and affection in her gentle Hawaiian voice. I knew that this elderly woman was the most profound impact on my life; I wondered if she would remember me from our brief encounters last year.

"Aloha! Welcome back to Hawai'i. I had a feeling you would return to see us."

"It would have been impossible for me to stay away from here. I'm so happy to be back; it feels like coming home." I went on to tell her how much I was enjoying the beauty and variety of Maui, and how each day here was an adventure of new discovery.

Mamma Lila asked me if I had gotten the chance to try snorkeling in Maui's crystal clear waters; she told me it was an experience I would not forget.

"I find snorkeling fascinating. I'd love to try it here in Hawai'i." To my surprise, Mamma Lila

said she knew an ideal spot near Lahaina, and that she would very much like to go with me. I felt honored to spend a day in the company of a lady such as Mamma Lila, and I had little hesitation in asking her, "Would tomorrow be too soon?"

"Tomorrow will be just fine," she replied.

The following morning, when I arrived at the Makuas', Mamma Lila was preparing a picnic basket for our outing. Soon, we were on our way, and after a short drive we arrived at Mile Marker Fourteen.

The road was close to the beach, and it was only a short walk through the kiawe trees to the sand. There were people here and there, spread out along the beach. Mamma Lila took my arm as she guided me around a turn in the shoreline to a more secluded area. I spread out the blanket and we settled down to enjoy the sights before us. I had barely spoken to Mamma Lila on our short drive over. She was so content and peaceful, my enjoyment of being with her was more than enough for me.

It wasn't one of Maui's best beaches, but for a novice like me, it was ideal. The water was calm and clear, containing an abundance of different species of multi-colored fish. Never have I experienced such an incredible day. The water

25

was warm and its beauty outstanding, as schools of exotic fish swam around me. I spent a couple of hours lost in the tranquility of the world below the ocean's surface. When I looked toward the beach, I could see Mamma Lila beckoning me and pointing towards the picnic basket.

We sat under the shade of a nearby tree enjoying our lunch. As we ate, I commented to Mamma Lila on Jonathan's casual attitude towards life and about his exuberance; for it was quite extraordinary and of a quality one does not meet every day.

Turning to me, she smiled. "At times, Jonathan is somewhat of a prankster and often treats life like an adventure. To him, the world is a playground, where he plays many roles, enjoying most of them. If I were you, Richard, I'd listen very carefully to him. That man knows more about the workings of the mind than any human being I know of at the present moment."

It was a little too much for me to hear Mamma Lila say that Jonathan knew as much, if not more than anyone in the universe about how the mind works. It was quite an extraordinary statement. "Tell me, Mamma Lila, how can Jonathan know so much when he has so little education? How is this possible?"

She looked straight into my eyes and without

the slightest hesitation said, "I realize Jonathan has very little education. He doesn't have a degree, but more importantly, he has a *connection*. Jonathan is what I would call a true theosophist. A true theosophist, really, is someone who doesn't talk from the learning process; he talks directly from the Source."

I shook my head in disbelief at what I was hearing, and yet Mamma Lila talked with such conviction. My mind drifted back to my days at the university, and I imagined how thrilling it would have been to sit in on a class with such a professor. The interest created would have had the whole academic community buzzing. And here I was now - blessed with the amazing good fortune to be granted the privilege of private conversations and even a close friendship with two such people.

"You know, I asked Jonathan the other day, 'How much do you know about the mind?' and he gave me the most unusual answer."

Mamma Lila looked at me with an amused expression, and raised her eyebrows. "Oh?"

"He said, 'If you took all that I know and put it in your eye, the best ophthalmologist in the country couldn't find it.'"

Mamma Lila looked at me and smiled.

"Mamma Lila, what do you think the average

27

person would have to say about this understanding of Jonathan's?"

"A lot depends on the evolution of the mind that is listening," she explained. "If the listener isn't ready, Jonathan's words would go over their head. People such as this would see Jonathan as denying or trying to destroy their beliefs, only to replace them with a different set of beliefs. On the other hand, a person fortunate enough to HEAR what Jonathan is saying would benefit immeasurably. He or she would realize that sanity - wisdom, common sense and love - lies at the core of every individual on earth."

"What do you mean by that?"

"He is telling you how to cultivate a deeper understanding of life. You see, Richard, *all* life is of spiritual essence, whether it be in form, or formless. When this spiritual essence takes form, we call it Nature. This form we call Nature has infinite separate realities, each reality being a fact to its observer. For example, the way you see life is your reality; therefore, we both see and live in separate realities. Do you understand what I'm trying to say?"

"Yes, I think so."

Mamma Lila then continued, "Although there are an infinite number of realities, there are only two worlds: the Spiritual and the Material. The

28

answer you seek is found when the two worlds become ONE."

Mana power, she told me, would give me the strength to break the limitations I had set on my life; limitations that had led me to the belief that what I saw was all that existed.

Then she said, "It is Mana power that makes the unknown, known."

She was most adamant about the fact that no one could explain the true meaning of Mana because it is of spiritual essence, and therefore non-tangible to our intellectual capabilities. "The secret of Mana cannot be given away, it is you who must find it."

"But how?" I pleaded.

Stretching out her arms in an embracing gesture, she said, "All you have to do is reach out and take what is yours by birthright!" Like Jonathan, Mamma Lila never appeared to give me a direct answer to any question.

Quick to notice the perplexed look on my face, she started to explain that what she spoke of was quite formless, "and being formless, it's impossible for the mind of humanity to visualize, because we live in a world of form."

Then, raising a single finger, she said, "One step beyond form lies the secret of the pearl of pearls. This is where the form and formless become *ONE*.

29

It is from here that the wise get their knowledge; from the *FORMLESSNESS* or great *NOTHING-NESS.*"

At first, I thought I understood what Mamma Lila was saying. Yet at the same time, it was obvious to me that I was not realizing the deeper meaning of her words.

"I'm afraid you've lost me somewhere in this conversation," I admitted. I honestly didn't understand what she was saying about form and formlessness, or how the wise get their power and wisdom from this "Great Nothingness." It was all very confusing to me! How could anyone get something from nothing?

My intellect balked at such oversimplification. To me, nothingness simply meant "zilch!" In her own gracious way, Mamma Lila then assured me that the nothingness I spoke of, and what she meant by *nothingness,* were two entirely different things.

At this point she cupped her hands and asked me what was in them.

"Nothing," I replied, "they are empty."

With a broad smile she said, "You mean 'zilch?' Wrong, there is air, as well as many more unseen forms." Waving her finger at me she said, "You see, you do *not* understand my meaning of nothingness."

30

I felt like I had on Kaua'i when she gave me the riddle about the palm tree. My stomach was like a tight ball as I waited for the trap to be sprung. I remembered Jonathan's warning that if I challenged her, I would find my world was built on a foundation of quicksand.

To my relief, Mamma Lila simply smiled, saying she never thought for a moment that I would understand what she meant about everything coming from a *formless* energy.

In a soft, gentle voice, she said, "My dear young man, there are many realities to see and many mountains to climb before you can understand such a statement."

My curious intellect made me wonder, and I asked, "What is the sense of understanding such a subject?"

Mamma Lila again surprised me by saying,

"It is knowledge such as this
that relieves the weary traveller
of his heavy burden in life.
It frees him from the bondage
of self-inflicted delusions.
It guides you to the
'Pearl of Wisdom' you seek."

"Tell me honestly, does such a pearl exist?"

"Of course it exists, otherwise I wouldn't be wasting my time talking about it, would I?"

I said nothing and waited for Mamma Lila to speak.

"The pearl you seek is cultivated just like any other pearl. The oyster tries daily to sweep away the unwanted impurities that irritate it. Consequently, a beautiful pearl is created from a grain of sand.

"Like the oyster you have to clean house every day. Then someday you might find your illustrious pearl. In other words, I am saying, be like the oyster and sweep away yesterday's impurities and free yourself from yesterdays!"

As she spoke, there was a gentleness and charisma about her that was undeniable. It had been another perfect day in paradise, and all too soon, it was time to drive Mamma Lila home.

Chapter
<u>4</u>

Beyond Ego Consciousness

Four days had passed since I last saw Jonathan. I'd really been looking forward to spending more time with him, so I arranged to meet my intriguing friend for lunch at a small restaurant in Lahaina. I felt very grateful for this man's friendship, and I wanted to ask him many questions. Something that had remained in my mind since my last visit was how emphatic Jonathan had been in refusing to defend and

debate his philosophical views on life.

I asked him not to regard my cross-questioning as a challenge, but rather as a result of my determination to uncover a deeper meaning of his words. Jonathan smiled at my statement, saying that perhaps if he could explain some of the pitfalls one is apt to fall into when living an argumentative life, it would help me understand what he meant, and why he refrained from engaging in arguments. With this, he started to relate a story.

"There was a certain gentleman called Charlie who was very proud of the fact that he had been taught to question, analyze, and argue as a way of life. His existence was one debate after another. Everyone he knew or met was a potential opponent he had to defeat. He walked through life a victim of society, not realizing that he had been taught to argue instead of to *listen*. This poor man got so lost in his argumentative reality he could find no peace of mind, and consequently experienced little or no love in his life. Everywhere he went, he found something to argue about, truly believing that this constant debate was a sign of intelligence. His friends and family, not relishing the idea of such foolish, unnecessary controversy, soon had less and less to do with him. Still, he couldn't *see* his folly.

34

"His confused and frightened state soon led him to try and find some relief through alcohol, which in turn led to marital problems. After years of arguing and fighting with his wife and family, a divorce was inevitable. This innocent person still couldn't see that he was judging everything in life. His mind had no resting place. With all his brilliant scholarly attainments, he had nothing of any tangible value for himself."

"That's a sad story, Jonathan. What happened to him?" I asked.

"Charlie soon began to lose control of his drinking and his life. Then one day, when he thought his life was finished and that it had all been in vain, he 'accidentally' came upon someone; someone who could *SEE* beyond his aggression and understand his folly. He had encountered a 'See-er.'

"Unknown to him, his final battle was about to begin. The battle field? A lonely bus stop. The See-er, armed with the invincible sword of wisdom, soon cut to pieces everything that was created from 'wrong thinking' and silly, nonsensical, argumentative behavior.

"It didn't take poor old Charlie long before he realized he had come upon an adversary who was quite different from anyone he was used to. Fear ran through him, as the See-er commanded,

35

'Look at what you are doing right now! *Listen to yourself!*'

"Magically, with those words, all fear vanished and in its place came a peaceful tranquility. As if awakened from a mesmerizing sleep, Charlie could *see* that his *own* thoughts, insecurities and competition were responsible for all the unnecessary suffering he had experienced throughout his life. At last, he had found the power to change his *thoughts*; he had found some true wisdom, which in turn freed him from the nonsense that had burdened him all of his life."

"That is a very moving story," I said, "but I can't understand why such an intelligent person couldn't see what he was doing. Surely, someone could have explained to him what was happening."

"It's not always that easy," Jonathan replied.

Perhaps it was something within me that his story had touched. "What eventually happened to Charlie?"

"He and his wife are together again, living a very happy life, now that he realizes that the understanding and love he was seeking were within himself all the time."

"Are you saying that because he *heard* one thing, it changed his whole life?"

"Yes, and much more than you could ever

36

imagine! This *hearing* assisted him to see beyond the misled reality he lived in. This simple realization brought with it the power to see and understand most of the silly, insecure habits he knowingly, or unknowingly, inflicted on himself and others, habits which had brought confusion and negative results into his own life.

> "Remember, it is *Thought*
> that leads to behavior.
> Change *Thought* and automatically
> the behavior will change.

"You know, Richard, there are many people who think in much the same way as Charlie. Because they were born into a poor family, they think that there isn't much chance for them in life. Truly, many believe: one birth, one death, and whatever happens in between is out of their hands. Being typical skeptics, they are full of disbelief, and remain on the same one way road going nowhere. To be honest with you, at one time I was in the same boat myself.

"Then one day I *heard* Mamma Lila speaking from a world I had not dared to even dream of. This realization made me see that the world Mamma Lila was speaking from was an inanimate world, a world of spirit; whereas I was

37

trying to figure out the animated human form. It was this simple realization that changed my life instantly, to one of deeper understanding. As if by magic, this simple experience started to reveal the mystical qualities of MIND and THOUGHT."

I told Jonathan it was an interesting story, but I wondered what he meant when he said Mamma Lila was speaking from an inanimate world.

"Now I don't want you to think that when I say 'Mamma Lila walks in another world,' I mean another world someplace else, 'Because there just ain't no place else to go!'"

Looking at my somewhat bewildered face, Jonathan casually remarked that another way to convey the same thing would be to say that Mamma Lila lives in a state of consciousness beyond the comprehension of most people.

"She is certainly a very fascinating lady," I said, "who at times, I admit, talks beyond my understanding. For instance, this talk about form and formlessness is very confusing! Do you understand such talk?"

Jonathan instantly broke into a little smile, then he again reminded me that I was looking for the unexplainable, and that I had fallen into the same old trap of listening only to Mamma Lila's words, while missing the essence of her story altogether!

"Do you mean I should guess what Mamma Lila

38

is saying?" I inquired.

After a few moments of silence, Jonathan said, "To guess would mean you didn't understand. It's not a matter of guessing, nor is it a matter of memorizing. Memorizing such words would be almost meaningless."

"What is it then?" I asked.

"It's a matter of *HEARING* with understanding that brings a positive *feeling*. This same positive feeling is the key that opens the door to all such knowledge."

"So what you are saying is that the secret of getting to know who and what we are, even the mystical secrets of life, will come via a positive *feeling*?"

Without the slightest hesitation Jonathan answered, "That's what I'm saying."

"I guess the important thing is to find a good teacher."

"Of course, good teachers are worth their weight in gold. We have wonderful places of learning, but you must be discriminating in choosing from all the various teachers out there. For instance, if I went to a teacher who told me that I could sit on a magic carpet and learn to fly, I would certainly want to see a demonstration. If the teacher couldn't do it, I'd have to say this was something like a bald man peddling hair tonic."

This brought to mind something I had heard about from a couple I knew back in New York, who were having problems with their marriage. Logic told them that their constant arguing would eventually lead to a divorce, which neither wanted. So they sought help, and were told to be 'up front' and unload all their anger and hostility towards each other. At first this technique sounded good. However, it didn't take them long to realize that what they were being told was not at all logical.

"The more they looked at their situation, the more they could see it was getting worse instead of better. Then one evening, the wife *saw* logic, and that there was no common sense in what she was being told. After all, both she and her husband had come to the therapy to find a way to *stop* arguing, and now they were being encouraged to fight with each other. It was like being asked to throw oil on a fire to extinguish it.

"That evening she and her husband walked out of a madhouse and returned to their home with sanity. To her, it was simplicity itself: the answer was *love*, and it was the lack of love that had created the misunderstandings and arguments in the first place. It was as if she was awakened from a nightmare. Her relief was overwhelming as she *KNEW* that her marriage was saved. This

new found love brought understanding beyond her wildest dreams and the beautiful long lost feelings she had for her husband returned.

"So strong was her love for him that soon all the silly, petty games they had played on each other ceased to exist, and the love and harmony they sought was theirs. The sad thing is that many who attended the awareness group never did see beyond their own dilemma, and I wouldn't be surprised if many of those poor souls are either separated or divorced today, or at least still arguing with each other."

Chuckling, Jonathan replied, "The trouble is, we have all been subjected to an overwhelming number of influences in our lifetime. This is why it is necessary to break one's thought patterns and go beyond the Ego Consciousness to perceive anything of real, practical, lasting value.

"Do you know something, Richard? One of the greatest discoveries you could realize is the mystical fact that the spiritual and the physical worlds are *One*. Only the form differs. This is what Mamma Lila was trying to explain to you, regarding form and formlessness."

Jonathan leaned back in his chair and gazed around the light and airy little restaurant. Scratching his head, he looked at me and said, "I'll try to explain this as clearly as I can, but remember,

41

I'm trying to explain the unexplainable."

"One world is spiritual, with no form, in-animate. The universe as we know it, with all of its contents, is animated. Here is where the dualism of life appears. It is this dualism that creates our folly because this is where humanity forgets its power to *Think* and succumbs to its own uncontrolled thoughts."

"I don't understand what you mean. Are you saying that I am leading myself on with my *own* thoughts and beliefs?"

Once again his answer was not as expected.

"The difference between wisdom and folly
is that fools know only what they think,
but the wise *know*
that they are the 'thinker.'
The difference between a wise man
and a fool is that
the wise man learns from a fool,
but a fool rarely learns from the wise.
Without Thought,
there wouldn't be an observer.
A *Thought* is what brings
consciousness into form.

"*Thought* is an obedient servant, obeying all commands. *Thought* is perpetual while conscious-

ness exists. It is the thinker who goes astray, not the *Thought*. When the thought system is jammed with imperfect thoughts, the system must create an imperfect realty. Again, I tell you, I am not saying who is right or wrong. I am simply explaining *Thought*, not the results of misleading Thoughts.

"The greatest folly of all, Richard, is what we think of ourselves and our own limitations. We don't realize that it is *Thought*, not *time* that brings about our evolution."

Jonathan's statement had the most peculiar effect on me. I experienced the feeling of deja vu, and for an instant, all the statements Jonathan had made about time which had been confusing to me came into clear focus. Jonathan, noticing my obvious excitement, said nothing and just sat back in his chair and smiled.

"Try and remember, I am *not* condemning anyone. I'm simply trying to explain something to you. It's a matter of evolution. When evolution takes place in this world, things change, and medieval ways disappear. It has always been this way and always will be.

"It's like this, Richard, a true genius in the field of psychology would understand the meaning of *Mind* and would be able to explain the connection between *Mind* and *Consciousness*. Such a person

43

would elevate the listener's understanding to a degree above and beyond that of their wildest imagination, bringing the secret of the original psychology, which by the way, is the study of *Mind* , *Soul* and *Spirit*. I want to make it perfectly clear I am *not* talking religion. I am simply telling you a few spiritual facts."

After lunch, we strolled back towards the seawall. For a long time, we sat quietly, watching the parade of splendid boats as they entered and left the picturesque little harbor of Lahaina. Looking around at the quaint buildings that were such a perfect blend of old and new, I had the feeling that this town had seen a lot of life.

Again, the heat from the sun was feverishly hot, and the day had turned into a scorcher. I suggested we have something refreshing to drink.

"Good idea," said Jonathan. We walked to a nice little place just around the corner, where we ordered two large, iced teas. As we sat, curiosity again got the better of me. I desperately wanted to know why Jonathan had commented earlier that any further discussion on ego would be fruitless. It really surprised me, because the last time I was in Hawai'i, we spoke freely for hours on this very subject. I asked him why he had changed his mind.

He looked at me with a very serious expression on his face. Then, after a long, thoughtful silence he said, "The last time you were here in Lahaina you were a different person. You saw life from another reality, so you perceived life quite differently from how you view it now! Don't you remember the last time I told you there were different levels of consciousness, and that each level was seeing and creating its own reality? Well, now it is time for you to take another journey, a journey into a deeper and more understanding reality."

Intrigued, I asked him what he meant by a journey into "another reality".

He pondered my question for a few moments, then adjusted his old straw hat. "A reality where 'ego' would have little or no power over you. I believe I told you before, to free oneself from the false illusions of 'ego' one has to realize what ego *Is*, not how it works.

"When one truly realizes what ego *Is*,
simultaneously one also finds out what it isn't.
When you find out what it isn't,
then you will be on your way
to the understanding you seek!"

It sounded like another riddle to me. At this

45

point, Jonathan casually looked at me and announced that I was as blind as a bat! "What do you mean by that?" I questioned indignantly.

With a look of utter glee on his face he said, "It's too late, you've already done it!"

"Done what?" I asked, mystified at his answer.

"Don't you *see*? You have already ventured into a reality superior to the one you lived in before your last visit to Hawai'i."

I wanted so much to understand him, and it was here that Jonathan's voice softened as he continued, "Don't you remember? When you arrived here on Maui before, your life was one of sickness, fear and hopelessness. You felt all was lost. Now you live in another reality altogether! Right?"

His words struck me like a bolt of lightning and chills ran all the way up my spine. Jonathan was right. My world had changed immeasurably since my last visit to Hawai'i.

My emotions again stirred and my eyes filled at the thought of being given this second chance in life. I was starting to realize to a deeper extent the significance of the gift I had been given. It wasn't too long ago that the thought of sharing my life with someone and having a family of my own was out of the question, but now it was all a distinct possibility. So much had changed, I could

not believe my good fortune.

"But how did it happen? To be honest with you Jonathan, sometimes I feel like I'm in the middle of a dream! There are so many questions I would like answered. What really happened to me the last time I was here?"

"I can't explain what happened to you, in the context from which you are asking. But I can tell you I've seen *many* people who have been touched by the same knowledge you en-countered. Once such knowledge has been seen, change in both the mind and body often occur. To a world unaccustomed to this Truth, the return to health will appear as an unexplainable miracle."

Now I began to understand why Jonathan had been so nonchalant when I first told him about my recovery. He went on, "I've seen many such miracles. Every day is a miracle. The very existence of Life itself is a miracle. So why should I be surprised when a miracle happened to you? Don't worry too much about what has gone on before. Just accept your good fortune, and never mind *why*."

Jonathan smiled, and said,

"Let's just say that you 'fell into a hole in time,' and if you just have patience, some of your answers might appear when you least expect

them. Then all the answers you get will be from your *own* inner wisdom, not from the falsehoods of others. I tell you my friend,

> Beware of cults and organizations,
> who talk a lot and say little.
> Beware of people
> who want you to follow them.

"Use the common sense you were born with. Never hand over your personal power to anyone, lest you lose your self esteem, which ironically is the very thing you seek."

Although Jonathan's words were simple, they echoed in my mind with a depth of meaning impossible to explain. I sat silently absorbing the powerful feelings that seemed to be filling the air all around us. Everything lightened, and I could feel a broad smile of gratitude spreading across my face. Jonathan's eyes met mine, with an expression of complete understanding.

After a time, my mind again came up with curious thoughts. I was about to try and delve deeper into Jonathan's philosophical views, but before I could open my mouth, he threw up his hands, "Please! Please, no more questions!"

Chapter 5

On Truth

The next few days were very quiet and peaceful. I spent hours at the hotel pool, enjoying the sunshine and cool water, watching the other vacationers relax and play. I would take refuge from the afternoon heat in the cool of my hotel room, appreciating the luxury of uninterrupted deep sleeps. The evenings were perfect for long walks on the beach. A beautiful crescent moon illuminated the night sky, and lent a picturesque

quality to the curving shoreline.

Returning to my hotel after a leisurely stroll, I decided to phone Mamma Lila and invite her to join me for dinner the following night. I had heard about a special little restaurant several miles up the coast in Napili, away from the hustle and bustle of Lahaina town. She accepted, and we agreed to meet an hour before sunset the following evening.

The next day was another one of peaceful relaxation. Late in the afternoon, I headed out for the Makuas' and met Mamma Lila. She was elegant and gracious, wearing a long old fashioned mu'u mu'u. A beautiful lei of delicate flowers and ferns encircled her head like a crown. She seemed to belong to another time. Her face shone, and I again felt very lucky to be spending time in the company of this charismatic, although somewhat inscrutable lady.

The drive up the coast was lovely. The vegetation was lush and green. The sun was low in the sky when we came to a small, crescent shaped wooden sign which read "Restaurant of the Maui Moon."

"Here we are," I said to Mamma Lila, as we pulled into a little parking lot, shaded by spreading monkeypod trees and palms. As if out of a dream, a quaint little entryway appeared at the edge of the greenery. It was shaped in an arch, in the Japanese style with shoji panelling. Low wooden benches

50

were on either side within the archway. Above, was the single word "Aloha."

I felt a shiver run through me as we walked through the entrance. We followed the pathway through the gardens, with the sea before us, and the sun sinking into the horizon like a golden ball. A walk across a grassy lawn brought us to the restaurant, which was nestled at one end of the bay on the sand's edge.

The view from our table was spectacular. We gazed out at the lovely curve of white sandy beach before us, glowing in the brilliant colors of sunset. Listening to the rhythmic pounding of surf on shore, I felt that I had truly found Paradise.

It was wonderful to sit and enjoy the beauty of the sunset with Mamma Lila. Her company, her total enjoyment of the experience, brought me a deep feeling of appreciation and gratitude for the scene before me.

Eventually, our dinner was served. We each had ordered the fresh "catch of the day," a fish with the local name "Ono," which means "good" or "tasty" in Hawaiian, and I must admit, it was a well named fish!

The sky darkened as we ate, and one by one the twinkling stars appeared. Mamma Lila, more than anyone I had ever met, had an innate wisdom, an understanding of life that seemed to emanate from

51

her. Yet her words were often more like riddles to me than answers.

In past conversations she had expressed the idea that everyone's truth was valid, yet she would also talk about "*The Truth*," as if there were one Absolute Truth. It was confusing to me, and I brought up the question, hoping for some insight.

"Mamma Lila, I find something hard to understand. If everybody's truth is true to them, how can there possibly be only one Truth?"

"That is a difficult question to answer directly," she said, with a thoughtful look on her face. "Perhaps if I relate a story, it will help you to understand. When I was a young girl, a very wise old Indian from Kansas visited my grandfather on the island of Lana'i. Our friend's arrival created great excitement on the island because few American Indians had been seen before by the residents. He was a very calm, carefree person, who, like my grandfather, had the power to *SEE* beyond our normal senses. As a young girl, I would listen to them speak about the mysteries of the universe. Each had a subtle sense of humor, and at times they would erupt into peals of laughter. Joseph, our guest, stayed with us for two months, and not once did I hear any kind of disagreement between him and my grandfather."

"That's quite unusual," I observed. "You would

think that with their different backgrounds they would differ on at least some of their philosophical views."

"Not really," replied Mamma Lila. "You see, they both *KNEW* they were talking the same *TRUTH*."

Pointing seaward, she said, "Call it the sea or call it the ocean... same thing!"

Her soft brown eyes returned to mine, as she said, "Everyone's truth is true to them. You see, Richard, within ourselves we have a magnificent gift; the gift of free thought. It is with this gift that we accept or reject whatever we see in life, and whatever we see in life is our personalized truth. This personalized truth has no stability. Like the trade winds, it can change from moment to moment, eventually ending up like old autumn leaves scattered in a windstorm.

"Now, there is a far greater Truth that is *impersonal*. This impersonal Truth is found within one's soul and is as steadfast as life itself. This is the *TRUTH* the wise have spoken of since the beginning of time. This is where they make their stand against all falseness of life. This *TRUTH* that I speak of is before the formation of thought or form, and when digested, it starts to unfold the mystical qualities of the world we live in."

Mamma Lila's words took my breath away. I was experiencing a beautiful feeling, like waves of

53

peace washing over me. For once, I had no desire
to say a word. We both gazed in silence at the
shimmering moonlit water. Above, a million stars
sparkled like diamonds. I had forgotten how clear
and beautiful the Hawaiian skies were.

A few minutes went by, then Mamma Lila said
"*TRUTH* is only abstract for those who disbelieve in
its existence. It is *TRUTH* that binds the spiritual
and material worlds together, bringing about a
common knowledge to all. It is the stepping stone
to the spiritual wonders which lie deep within our
consciousness."

This petite lady never ceased to astonish me with
her unique logic. After some time, Mamma Lila
continued her story, saying that the last evening
spent with Joseph was one of the most memorable
experiences of her life. She recalled, "The love that
emanated from those two gentle souls was
extraordinary. I remember Joseph reaching into his
pocket and pulling out a bracelet that had been
given to him by his mother. 'Here, little one,' he
said to me. 'Take this and wear it always. It may
help you to find what you seek.' Then, he fastened
the bracelet on my wrist. As a little girl, I wore the
shiny bracelet with great pride. My grandfather
later explained that Joseph had paid me a great
honor by giving me his prize possession."

She glanced down at her wrist where she still

wore the bracelet. I could see by the look on her face how she treasured the gift and her memories of Joseph. Looking at it closely, I could see some Indian carvings on it with the simple inscription:

"LOVE-SPIRIT-SOURCE"

"I remember asking Joseph why people found it so difficult to live in harmony, and why they had to continually fight instead of living in the Aloha spirit.

"Joseph replied,

'Sometimes our eyes
are blinded by the mist
which stops us
from seeing the horizon.'"

As she spoke, the power radiating from this unique lady was almost too much to behold.

It was then that Mamma Lila started to explain that there are invisible veils surrounding everyone's realities, and this is one of the main reasons why we have such difficulty under-standing each other's ideas and ways. "If you can learn to draw away this curtain of ignorance, you will uncover the secret of separate realities, or as Jonathan would put it, 'The logic of MIND.'"

Again I was overwhelmed by the feeling behind the words Mamma Lila was speaking.

We sat for the longest time in silence, then Mamma Lila said, "Try looking at it this way, Richard. Life on earth is a spiritual game of *Thought*, Thought being the divine bridge between the known and unknown.

"It is *Thought* that bridges the spiritual and material worlds together, bringing the knowledge you seek.

"This is why I say to you: If your thoughts and your heart lack the Aloha feeling, then you will see and live in a world of confusion. On the other hand, if your heart is filled with the Aloha Spirit, then your bridge of thought will be strong and healthy, leading you to a stable life."

I had never heard "*Thought*" described in such a way before, and it intrigued me. I asked Mamma Lila, "What about the power of thought and the power of our minds? How do they work together?"

"They are inseparable," she replied.

In the silence that followed, a question came to my mind. "Mamma Lila, what do you mean when you talk about 'Aloha?'"

"Aloha means many things. In this part of the world, as you know, it is used to welcome someone or to bid them farewell, but it also means much more than that; Aloha is *Love*.

56

"The Aloha Spirit is both the essence and strength of our Hawaiian heritage. Without it, we would be like children lost in the dark. The graceful pride of our people is a natural expression of Aloha. We have truly been blessed with a priceless gift, and it is ours to share.

"The Aloha Spirit is what helps to guide us through life, keeping us in harmony with nature and our fellow human beings. One cannot express true Aloha on an intellectual basis, because it is a *feeling* that comes directly from the heart. It is a way of life; knowing intuitively what to do and when to do it, giving without thought of return or fear of need, with great faith in the abundance of life.

"Aloha has sometimes been defined in this way: 'A' signifies light or enlightenment. 'Lo' means close to the earth, and 'Ha' is the living breath of the Creator. By this definition, Aloha means 'Enlightenment on this earth through the breath of the Creator.'

"It is said that the truly wise see not the form, but the formless, seeing each other as the true Aloha Spirit, encased in human form. Aloha is another way of saying, 'I see God in you and you see God in me. We are One 'Ohana, One Family.'"

As Mamma Lila spoke, feelings I had never experienced before were filling me, to the point

57

where chills ran through me and tears came to my eyes. The feelings were too strong for my mind to analyze. They were so beautiful, the only thought I had was "Thank you."

<u>Chapter 6</u>

A Hole in Time

All too rapidly my vacation was nearing an end and I now felt every moment left in Hawai'i was precious. I had arranged to meet Jonathan to take a drive up to Ka'anapali.

He picked me up early at my hotel and we headed out. As we slowly made our way down Front Street in Lahaina I had to ask Jonathan to explain a phrase he had used the other day, regarding the disappearance of my illness.

59

"Jonathan, the other day you said I was lucky inasmuch as I had fallen through a hole in time. The idea fascinates me. To be honest, it sounds like nonsense. I wonder if you could explain to me what you meant."

Stroking his chin, Jonathan appeared deep in thought. "Have you ever heard it said that some people are ahead of their time?"

"You mean inventors, like Bell and Edison?"

"Precisely. They were definitely men who were ahead of their time."

At this point he stopped talking and glanced out the window towards the sea. I waited patiently for him to explain further, but he just drove on with a twinkle in his eye, as if he were baiting me. Finally, I couldn't restrain myself any longer.

"I'm starting to get an inkling of what you mean, but I'm still mystified by the idea of a 'hole in time.' Could you try and enlighten a New York dummy?"

Smiling, Jonathan adjusted his old straw hat and gave a huge sigh. "By the way, before I answer your question, have you still got that little tape machine of yours?"

"Yes, it's in my satchel."

"I advise you to get it out. I have a strong feeling you might need it today!"

I couldn't help recalling how many of Jonathan's answers went by me before I had a chance to grasp

60

them. Once, when he'd been explaining something, I started taking notes, but he looked at me as if I were crazy. "How on earth do you expect to *Hear* anything I'm saying if you're busy trying to write it all down? You'd be two sentences behind me all the time, rushing to catch up, copying down empty words without any idea of the true meaning behind them."

He'd shaken his head and begun to smile, but I'd had trouble finding the humor in the situation. Seeing this, Jonathan patted me on the back and said gently, "Don't worry about remembering what's being said. It really doesn't matter. The answer comes in the *feeling*, not the words."

I was only now starting to recognize the truth of his statement. The beautiful, life-changing experiences I'd had since meeting Jonathan and Mamma Lila were definitely brought about by *feelings*, and had nothing to do with my intellectual understanding of their words. In fact, when these feelings came, my intellect had usually been left far behind, having given up even trying to comprehend the words.

Reaching for my cassette player, I explained to Jonathan how I appreciated being able to record his words. By now we were outside of Lahaina driving north. Jonathan slowed down as we approached a beautiful little beach park, separated

61

from the road by colorful hedges of pink and red bougainvillaea. He turned into the entrance, and we agreed to continue our conversation on the grass, looking out over the waves. Gentle breezes cooled us, and I again marveled at the splendor of Maui.

Once we were settled again, Jonathan continued, "First of all, you will have to realize that time has nothing to do with Wisdom or the true evolution of the mind of humanity. That is a fallacy. Evolution of the mind takes place in a timeless state, beyond the realm of time. Some people call this an insight, or, if you wish, a sight from within.

"When Bell had his *realization*, his consciousness visualized what is now called a telephone."

"What does consciousness have to do with thought?"

"You can't have consciousness without thought, or thought without consciousness. Thought is just as constant as consciousness. It's like this, Richard: there are two thought systems, the Divine, and the personal. Bell entered the Divine thought system for a split second when he had his realization."

His explanation fascinated me to no end. "But I'm afraid I still don't get the connection between Bell's telephone and a hole in time."

"I just told you. You're not *Listening*. Blow that cosmic wax out of your ears and *Listen*; I'll explain

again.

"At the precise moment Bell realized his vision, a spiritual path was cleared and from the unknown he *Saw* his beloved telephone. His mind had dropped all worldly thoughts. He was neither in the past nor were his thoughts in the future, and from this point, using thought as a vehicle, the unknown became known."

Jonathan grinned from ear to ear, and I couldn't contain my own amusement at the way our conversation seemed to be going around in circles.

Earlier, Jonathan had stated that there was more than one natural state of evolution. This had been news to me, and I had to ask him what he had meant.

He slowly shook his head from side to side, "When you were a little boy, didn't your mother tell you not to try and bite off any more than you could chew?"

"I guess most mothers tell their kids that!"

"Well, I'm saying it again to you, only this time you must try and digest food for thought, before asking more questions." He continued with his explanation.

"One form of evolution is what we call 'natural,' the other I spoke of is a step higher into the 'superior natural.' The natural evolution is of the mind of humanity, governed by Time and Thought.

This only unveils more intellect, and causes history to repeat itself."

"The 'Superior evolution' is unveiled in a Timeless state. It is in this state of *THOUGHT* that all wisdom comes forth to the world. When it arrives, it comes from a reservoir of mystical knowledge that lies in the heart of all humans."

From my previous trip to Hawai'i, I had come to feel that Jonathan was a very deep person, as well as a highly colorful human being. Only now was I beginning to realize just how extraordinary a man I had bumped into in this life!

We sat for awhile, hypnotized by the sight of sparkling blue ocean rolling toward the shore, and entranced with the beauty of waves crashing on rocks and sand. Grey clouds passed across the sun and a gentle rain descended upon us, so we returned to the car.

As we continued on our drive, the sun shone through the mist, creating spectacular arches of rainbows around us. The sky cleared again to a beautiful blue as we reached our destination - a long stretch of white sandy beach.

We spent a timeless afternoon swimming, sunning and walking along the shore, entertained by the sight of children and families enjoying themselves in the waves. As the sun dropped close to the horizon, a stillness seemed to cover

everything. The winds died down, the waves became gentle, and we were caught in a moment of eternity as the golden ball disappeared into the sea.

Vibrant, pastel colors filled the sky as we headed towards a little pool-side cafe in front of a nearby hotel, where we had a delicious evening meal.

Finally, we strolled back down to the ocean. We sat under the swaying palms, and drank in the magnificent view. The lights from the hotel next door lit up the beach, creating the dramatic appearance of golden sand. A full moon illuminated the glistening water. Our conversations and the experiences of the day had brought me new feelings, and my senses felt sharper and more alive. Life was starting to take on a different appearance to me, and I said to Jonathan, "Most of us really don't have a clue of what life is all about, do we?" I couldn't help but smile. "That's quite a predicament. Why do you think that is?"

Looking at me for a split second, he replied, "THOUGHT. JUST THOUGHT."

The simplicity of his answer caught me off guard, and he knew it. He started laughing so hard, he seemed to be doubled up in pain. I'd heard Jonathan have many a good belly laugh, but tonight there was no stopping him. We rose to return to the car and every few steps we took walking back to the parking lot, he would look at

65

me and burst into hysterics. Although I didn't quite understand what he found so funny, it didn't take long before I was laughing right along with him.

It truly was one of the craziest evenings of my life. There I was, standing in the middle of a parking lot laughing my head off without even knowing why - but it sure felt good.

Eventually our hilarity subsided, and we both took a final look at the incredibly peaceful scene before us. At last we reached the car and soon were heading towards Lahaina. I told Jonathan how much I had enjoyed the entire day; the talk, and especially the good laugh.

We drove on in silence, except for the sound of the rush of air outside the car. As we sat there, my thoughts kept returning to the intellect, and how it seemed as if what Jonathan called "True Knowledge" was not connected with the intellect, or related to how "smart" a person is. I had always thought that knowledge and intellect went hand in hand; I couldn't see where the idea of what Jonathan referred to as 'realization' fit in either, and I said as much to him.

"My friend," he replied, "Remember the experience you had talking with the consultant at your company? What happened was you slipped into a deeper reality, and that's what gave you that

extra bit of understanding. If the consultant had had the same understanding, he would have been cured. You see, Richard, when a true realization takes place, it's not the knowledge from one's intellectual understanding, rather, it's a glimmer from the spiritual intelligence that guides one's direction from *within*. When this kind of insight takes place, you should never fear its arrival. It comes not like the roar of a lion, but gently, like a lamb, bringing contentment and positivity. It is *never* disturbing. Such a realization comes from a source of uncontaminated knowledge.

"It is the simplicity of such knowledge that defies our intellectual understanding. This is why, when you seek such knowledge, you must be prepared to drop the misguided thoughts that contaminate your life at present."

Turning to me, he said, "People who are unprepared to give up a negative way of thinking for a more positive way remind me of a story.

"Once upon a time a man noticed that his shoes were getting old and shabby, yet he thought that if they had lasted him this long, they'd last a lot longer. Anyway, he was *attached* to them and it wasn't until one day when he noticed a big hole in his right shoe that he decided to do something about it, so he sought out the local shoe store. After making his purchase, he walked out of the store

and up the street, with great pride in his new right shoe. Tucked under his arm was the box containing one old shoe and one new. Delighted at having replaced the old 'holy' right shoe, he never even noticed the dilapidated condition his other shoe was in."

The picture of such a scene tickled my sense of humor, and I couldn't help but smile. Jonathan too seemed quite amused at the thought.

"It's like life: we tend to hang onto our old bad habits and ways of thinking, even after coming across a better way! Often, to no avail, we try to mix oil and water.

"You know, Richard, people think they can blend their old way of thinking with newly found knowledge. I can assure you of the impossible task of trying, yet it would surprise you how many people are walking around this world today wearing one old shoe, and one new."

<u>Chapter</u>
<u>7</u>

Beliefs vs True Knowledge

It was a short and pleasant walk from my hotel to the old stone wall fronting Lahaina Library, where I had arranged to meet Jonathan. I was a little early, and Jonathan was nowhere in sight. It was a beautiful sunny morning, and already Lahaina was buzzing with tourists.

Lahaina seems to be one of those special little towns that attracts people, perhaps because of its uniqueness. There are quaint shops all along the

69

main street, with windows displaying scrimshaw, jade and coral jewelry, beautiful tropical paintings and posters, as well as prints depicting the people and way of life of old Hawai'i. The whole atmosphere surrounding Lahaina gave me a feeling of timelessness. Waiting for Jonathan, I sat watching the pageantry of people passing by. Many of them, I imagined, were very grateful to be here on Maui. It was a beautiful morning. The sea was still and there was just a suggestion of a soft breeze.

The harbor activity increased as boat owners started to ready their crafts for sea. There were boats to satisfy everyone; boats to take you fishing, boats for sight-seeing, glass bottomed boats to tour the coral reefs offshore, and boats to take you whale watching. Time drifted by as I watched the tourists preparing to board, especially the children, some of whom were fairly dancing with excitement.

As I sat there, I couldn't help but think back on my first visit to Lahaina. It all seemed so dreamlike and unreal. Over and over again, my mind wondered about how fate had led me to this very wall, where I had first met Jonathan, and how his mystical presence had fascinated me beyond anything I had ever experienced.

I will never forget the way he conversed, taking

me totally by surprise, dumbfounding me to the point where my intellect just couldn't cope with it. So many times since then, I had tried to explain to my friends the impact Jonathan had on me, but always I was met with disbelief and skepticism. Whenever I think about the mysterious disappearance of the cancer from my body, even I find it hard to relate to.

At times, I've wondered if it were all just a figment of my imagination. What was it about Mamma Lila and Jonathan that made them so different from others? I'd often tried to figure it out, but always to no avail.

As I sat there on the wall, all I could do was feel extraordinarily grateful, and shake my head in wonder. I remembered one time, when Jonathan and I had been sitting on that same seawall, and he had said to me that a person such as Mamma Lila was invisible to the general public, and only those who were ready, had the eyes to *see* her and the ears to *hear*. Such mystical statements were quite typical of Jonathan.

I'd asked him what he meant, thinking at first that he was saying people couldn't physically see or hear Mamma Lila. Later, I realized Jonathan's *seeing* and *hearing* were of a metaphysical nature. I was no different from most people who encountered Jonathan and Mamma Lila, thinking that

71

they were simply two ordinary people, whose philosophical views were just another set of ideas and concepts. However, now I realize there is more to them than meets the eye. As yet, I can't explain what it is. All I know is, when one truly LISTENS to them, their words start to unravel a deeper insight into life than one could ever imagine, bringing spiritual insights that have the power to change the unpleasant situations of life to pleasant ones.

At that particular time, I had asked Jonathan, "Why is it that some people can't *hear*, and others can?"

"Simply because some are ready, and others are not," he replied. "Those who can't, haven't evolved enough. Such a person's journey in life is incomplete!" Then he said, "Trouble is, many look in the wrong direction for the answer they seek. Some look west instead of east!"

"I'm afraid I don't quite understand. Can you explain it another way?"

Jonathan had smiled and said, "Sure. Some face north instead of south."

"That's no clearer an answer than your last one!" I'd protested.

"You are trying to figure it all out intellectually. I've told you before, the *hearing* and *seeing* I speak of is beyond the already formed intellect. Just *listen*

and the answer you seek will come to you."

I couldn't help but tell Jonathan that sometimes his answers didn't make sense. He immediately burst into laughter, stating that as far as he was concerned, his answers made perfect sense, and it was only me who was hearing non-sense!

"OK," I had persisted, "Tell me again what you really mean by *hearing* and *seeing* in comparison to simply hearing and seeing intellectually."

"Hearing and seeing," he said, "comes from your already formed, intellectual understanding that is already computed in your old noggin." He pointed to my head. "It is what you would call one's natural process of thinking.

"On the other hand, the mystical HEARING and SEEING comes not from the intellect, but from deep within your very soul.

"It is knowledge that exists before time immemorial, knowledge that is waiting to be released as an insight, or, if you will, a spiritual revelation.

"Remember, my dear young man, LIFE is spiritual, turned into physical, and controlled and operated by your own free-will and thought system. It is your own free-will and thought system that has led you astray. Now! If you can go back to the ORIGINAL Divine Thought System, you will learn to SEE and HEAR anew."

I was about to question his third answer, when he raised his hand to indicate, "Enough!"

"Young man, you are not LISTENING. May I suggest you go home and figure these answers out on your own."

We had sat looking at the moonlit ocean for a short while, then Jonathan said he'd like to head home, as it had been a very long day for him. We shook hands and promised to meet the following morning. Jonathan took a few steps, then began laughing his head off, knowing he had left me completely confused. At that point, I was starting to realize what Mamma Lila had meant when she told me that Jonathan was quite a prankster.

Remembering that evening, I gazed out again at the beautiful glistening waves, and thanked God for the fullness I was feeling. Jonathan and Mamma Lila had given me so much. How it had happened, I couldn't begin to explain, but I knew I would be grateful to them for the rest of my life.

"Fascinating scene, isn't it?" I turned to see my friend Jonathan beside me.

"Hello, Jonathan! How long have you been sitting here?"

"Just a few seconds," he replied. We sat together quietly for a time, enjoying the sights and sounds before us.

A group of children had gathered in front of a

74

beautiful old square rigged sailing ship. One boy, about six, called out to an older man on deck, "Are you a pirate?"

Adjusting his sea captain's hat, he sauntered over toward the rail. "Why? You lookin' to sign up as crew?"

"Yeah!" the youngster shouted eagerly, echoed by a chorus of "Yeah! Me too!" from the others. The captain slowly looked them over, then with a wink, he said gruffly, "Ah, you gang are a bit puny yet - come back in a few years and we'll set out for a real adventure. I hear there's treasure hidden somewhere in them thar waters - diamonds! By the bucketful, I'm told."

Jonathan and I chuckled at the scene. I told him it reminded me of a time when I was about twelve and we went to Disneyland for a vacation. My favorite part had been the "Pirates of the Caribbean."

"You know Richard, I've never been there, though I'd love to go someday." After a pause he continued, "I think Walt Disney was one of the greatest men America has ever known. He taught the world to dream. He taught children from one to one hundred how to use their imaginations. He brought humanity a lot of love. When his countrymen needed him, he served them well, in his own unique way. That's one American I take

75

my hat off to. Without dreams we really have nothing, and he taught millions the possibility of dreams coming true."

I'd never heard Jonathan speak quite so wistfully. I asked him, "Do you really believe in dreams coming true?"

He looked me straight in the eyes for several seconds before he replied, "You should believe in them, Richard. Yours came true, didn't they? Weren't you healed? Didn't you find some peace of mind? Didn't you get a second chance in life?"

My chest swelled as if it was going to burst, as I responded, "Yes, it's true."

We silently gazed at the scene before us for several minutes before Jonathan spoke again. "Pretty soon my house is going to be torn down to make way for a shopping center."

I was startled at the news. I knew Jonathan would miss the quiet of his home. "I'm sorry to hear that."

He turned to me with his gentle smile, "It's not as bad as it sounds. It's giving me the opportunity to see more of this incredible country we live in. I'm ready to leave the Islands, to experience some of the other beautiful places that are waiting out there.

"I'd love to see the Rocky Mountains again, and I'm looking forward to doing some fishing in a lake or stream. As a matter of fact, trout fishing used to

76

be my way of relaxing; never caught much but sure enjoyed it. And I'd like to see my sons and their families again."

The thought of Jonathan wandering around without a permanent home of his own concerned me to no end. "Won't it trouble you not having somewhere to hang your hat?"

With a shrug of his shoulders Jonathan replied, "Perhaps some day I will find the right place to 'hang my hat,' but right now I have things to do and places that I would like to see before I die." With a twinkle in his eye Jonathan jestured towards the shoes he was wearing and remarked that a few years back he had received a very special gift. "With this gift came these old vagabond shoes, and now it feels like time I started to use them."

It was hard for me to imagine what Maui would be like without Jonathan. He was so much a part of my experience of the Islands. Jonathan rose and started walking towards the docks, gazing up at the riggings of the old fashioned sailing vessel moored there. He was only a few steps away when suddenly I had the strangest feeling, a feeling that I would never see him again once he left Hawai'i. Shaking the thought from my head, I joined him.

"You know, Jonathan, I was reminiscing before you came, about the state I was in when we first met, and how you somehow helped me find life

again when I was expecting to die of cancer. There was no way I could explain what happened to any of my friends back in New York.

"One of my closest friends, who I had known for years, had the most unusual reaction. When I'd been sick, he had spent hours with me, trying to cheer me up, and pointing out the brighter things in life. As soon as I heard the cancer was gone, he was the first one I went to see. Well, when I told him the incredible news that I was cured, he said very casually, 'These things happen, people do change,' and that was it! He gradually faded from my life, and the times we did spend together, he acted like nothing at all had happened! He never brought up the subject again, and stopped calling me."

Jonathan was silent for a moment. "Perhaps the power of your experience was just too much for him to face, in spite of his friendship. People react to mysteries like this in different ways."

I thought it had something to do with beliefs, so I asked Jonathan what he thought the difference was between our beliefs and what he called "True Knowledge."

After a long silence, he said, "There is quite a difference between beliefs and *True Knowledge*. A belief is only a temporary assumption whereas *True Knowledge* is what puts life into otherwise lifeless

wishes. It expands the boundaries of the ego mind and its assumptions, bringing with it a deeper understanding of the principal workings of MIND and THOUGHT."

"That's a fascinating theory," I countered, "but what about its practicality? Throughout time people have claimed to have found an insight into a deeper knowledge, and then find they cannot explain it, or prove to others that it actually exists - of what value is it then?"

Jonathan sat for what seemed an interminable time. Then he agreed that such knowledge could not be proven, that it had to be *SEEN* and *HEARD* via an experience. That is why such knowledge was often referred to as a "secret" or "hidden" knowledge. "But don't get me wrong," Jonathan added, "It's not a secret that I wouldn't want to tell you. Neither I nor anyone else can communicate *True Knowledge* with mere words because it's not an intellectual hearing. Rather, it's a *hearing* beyond your intellectual understanding. A realization is the opening of the intellectual gate beyond which lies the power of *True Knowledge*."

Jonathan's answers always fascinated me. I began telling him that I was well acquainted with all of my beliefs, and that I couldn't imagine my own beliefs hiding anything from me.

Without hesitation Jonathan said, "As a matter of

fact, such Knowledge is so well hidden that even people who have had a direct experience, like yourself, often fail to SEE the power behind the existence of such knowledge."

His words pierced my heart like a sword and for some unknown reason I found myself on the defensive. But before I could gather my thoughts together to say anything, Jonathan leaned towards me in a secretive manner and said, "Don't worry, you aren't the only one in this world who has failed to *SEE* what happened to him. True Knowledge can be somewhat mystifying when first encountered, and one is very apt to intellectually dismiss it as another theory, instead of looking for a deeper dimension of THOUGHT."

He continued, "It takes courage to have another look at the whole situation, and to see that the key to such a reversal lies in positive thought. If one perceives life in a positive manner, this alone will help bring about a deeper understanding of life. Of course, it goes much deeper than simple 'positive thinking.'

"Negative thoughts, on the other hand, turn life into hell and torment with no chance of relief. Beware when you are told that it is beneficial to work out your anger and hostilities."

"Don't you believe it's beneficial to get your anger and hostilities out rather than bottling them up

In Quest of the Pearl

inside?" I queried.

Jonathan replied, "Venting one's anger, and understanding the cause of the anger, are two different things altogether. People who insist on venting their anger remind me of a highly pressurized steam vessel that releases automatically at a dangerous pressure; however, as long as the fire remains under the vessel, the same ongoing danger exists. So one must learn to extinguish the fire, the fire in this case being one's own misguided *THOUGHTS* such as greed, anger, hate, desire, jealousy, fear, despair, or any other negative feeling that stops us from finding the understanding and peace we seek."

There was a long pause, then Jonathan remarked that he had met almost every type of person on earth and to this day he had never met an angry person who lived a happy life. He said that it made him shudder to think of how many innocent people had been told it was beneficial to argue and fight with their spouses and friends. No wonder there were so many divorces and broken friendships.

One thing was for sure, Jonathan was speaking the truth when he said the divorce rate had spiraled in the past few years, while at the same time this approach to letting anger out had become more common. I sat contemplating his words with an

intense interest and couldn't help agreeing with
him.

Very casually, Jonathan said,

> "The way you act in life
> is directly related to the way you *Think*.
> If you think negative, logic says
> you must act and feel negative.
> On the other hand, if you think positive,
> you will feel, see, and act positive.
> It's like the old saying
> 'What you give you will receive.'
> This law cannot be broken.

"Historically, whenever true knowledge has been
revealed it has always been lost, due to the fact that
many people honestly and sincerely believe they
hear and understand what is being said, when in
fact their personal interpretations of that *TRUTH*
have taken them far from it."

"That may very well be the fact in some cases," I
replied, "however I feel that all our truths differ
somewhat according to our culture and heritage."

At this point Jonathan surprised me when he let
me know in no uncertain terms that I was talking
personal truth and he was talking *universal*. He
wholeheartedly agreed that "all personal truths
differ," but that universal *Truth* never varies.

82

Shaking his head from side to side he added, "I'm afraid that all the discussions Mamma Lila had with you regarding *TRUTH* were in vain."

I felt truly remorseful after hearing his observation.

"I don't know whether you know it or not, but you are the only one I know of in two years to whom Mamma Lila has taken the time to explain the precious secret that she possesses. Why she picked you, I don't really know, but the one thing I know for sure is that you are a lucky young man.

"When I told you that Mamma Lila came here to see her long time friends Mr. and Mrs. Makua, I didn't tell you the whole story about her visit to Maui. The greater truth is that she is here to say good-bye to her friends, because she knows she is dying and her end is near."

I was shocked, and stood motionless as the meaning of Jonathan's words sank in.

Slowly I asked, "What's wrong with her?"

"Don't rightly know. All I know is, those of us who got to know her are the lucky ones. It's not every day you meet someone with the wisdom and knowledge she possesses. As a matter of fact, should you search this whole wide world, I doubt that you would ever find another with her incredible love and understanding."

I guess the expression on my face revealed my

feelings of sorrow. Jonathan, laying his hand on my shoulder, expressed, "Two things cannot be avoided... life and death."

Jonathan's words hit me hard. I had a sinking feeling in my stomach, and a fear that I had forever lost a golden opportunity. At the same time, a gentle feeling of awe and wonder came over me, a feeling of gratitude at having met such people as Jonathan and Mamma Lila.

<u>Chapter</u>
<u>8</u>

Mind

That evening as I was relaxing in my hotel room, I received a call from Jonathan, telling me that we'd been invited upcountry to a family picnic the next day. It was to be a small get together for Mamma Lila, given by her family and close friends. I felt that the invitation was a true privilege, and eagerly accepted.

The following afternoon Jonathan came to pick me up and we headed out on the highway. The

changing scenery and the natural splendor of the cliffs and mountains on the one side, crystal blue ocean on the other, was spectacular in the brilliant sunshine. Lilting Hawaiian music coming from the car radio enhanced the visual beauty surrounding us, creating an experience of near perfection as we drove along.

Something had been in the back of my mind for awhile now. I couldn't seem to grasp what Jonathan meant by his use of the word '*Mind.*' "Jonathan," I asked, "you use the word '*Mind*' differently than most people. What is it that you are referring to?"

He glanced over at me, and said, "It's not the personal mind as we call it in our culture, but the Master-Mind, and it is via this Master-Mind that all intelligence comes into being. The *Master-Mind* is what the mystics of the world would call 'Source.'"

Jonathan pondered for a few moments, then started to explain how in reality there is only one *MIND*, and that it is the *Master-Mind*, and this is the reason See-ers of the world consider the ego-mind to be of little or no value.

For some unknown reason, this struck a chord, and I remembered my university days when I once read that the vast majority of researchers believed that consciousness could be ignored insofar as the study of the mind is concerned. I mentioned this to

Jonathan.

"Yes," replied Jonathan, "I'm fully aware of that point of view, but the important thing is not how other people feel about the subject, but how YOU feel about it. Never mind trying to quote or memorize other people's ideas. A great part of our problem is that we are taught to constantly quote others, giving very little credit to our own inner wisdom. Look what happened to you," he went on, "you graduated with honors as a chattering parrot; a parrot who forgot how to think for himself." With this, his face sparkled with mirth.

I didn't find Jonathan's statement as amusing as he did, but I had to admit that it brought a funny picture to mind. Grinning from ear to ear he said, "Do you honestly believe what you are saying about *MIND*?"

"I'm not sure," I replied hesitantly. "The Mind is a subject that has occurred to me from time to time, but as far as I am concerned it is a very obscure topic to discuss."

"It sure is," agreed Jonathan, "especially when you don't know or care what it is. Such a statement as you don't have to acknowledge the existence of *MIND*, is ludicrous, to say the least."

Jonathan again had stirred something in me that captured my imagination. I asked if he could explain in some other way what he believed Mind

to be.

He paused momentarily, then started to tell me how it was an impossible task to explain the secret of *MIND* because, "It's a secret! Let me remind you again, don't listen to the words! At times words are used to try to express the inexpressible. It's like this, Richard, most of the trouble lies in the fact that the See-ers of the world have no other choice but to try to express their meaning by using allegorical or metaphorical explanations, which are often misinterpreted as a reality, thereby misguiding the listener.

"However, those who have learned to *LISTEN*, hear not the words, but the meaning *beyond* the words. It is understanding such as this that will uncover for you the correlation between *THOUGHT* and *MIND*."

It was here that I asked Jonathan where he thought the brain fitted into the picture. He answered by saying that as far as he could see, the brain is a biological organ, which stores all past and present experiences, and works on the same principle as any other computer, which is whatever is put into the memory bank is all that can be recalled.

"The brain, as any doctor will tell you, is an extremely complicated organ, and like all other complicated computers, can malfunction for one

reason or another. This is where the experts such as neurosurgeons come into the picture. Skillfully, they try to repair the human computer. However, this is where the brain and *MIND* separate; the simple reason being, the brain is physiological, whereas *MIND* is of a spiritual, non-physical nature."

Looking at me, his eyes sparkled as he said, "I have a strong feeling that at times you think I am not answering your questions, but believe me, I am. That is why I tell you, you will never find the answer you seek within the graveyard of your own thoughts and memories."

"If it's as easy and as simple as you're telling me, why is it that no one has heard those wise people?"

Jonathan smiled as he said, "Many people suffer from the very common ailment known as the cosmic earwax syndrome, and if you're not careful, it could be terminal. As a matter of fact, there are people who wander from the cradle to the grave and never *HEAR* one single worthwhile thing in life. Just like you," he said, "ears packed solid."

As we came to a stop sign, Jonathan pulled the car to a halt, leaned over, and proceeded to examine my ear. With a chuckle he stated that my prognosis was not too hot!

We drove through the busy districts of central Maui, and onto the clear expanse of highway

leading upcountry. Rolling pasture lands dotted with cattle, horses, and even some sheep, eventually gave way to vast acres of pineapple fields, stretching out on either side of the road. Haleakala filled the sky before us, strikingly clear in the late afternoon sunlight. Turning off the highway, we headed up a winding road which took us above the pineapple fields. Beautiful shade trees lined the way, some with unusual orange flowers, some covered with yellow blossoms. Through the trees we caught glimpses of the ocean, deep blue contrasting against the green fields stretched out below.

At the crest of the hill, we approached the spacious grounds of an old plantation home. A massive jacaranda tree graced the front lawn, its bright purple flowers dancing lightly on the breezes, its branches like a great canopy of purple velvet, providing shade to the small group of people below. Quite a few cars were parked in the driveway, so we left ours in front and began walking up the path toward the house.

The scene before us was picturesque: colorfully dressed people relaxing and laughing together beneath the trees, happy children running and playing on the grass. Heart shaped anthuriums and exotic bird of paradise flowers mixed with other lovely plants and ferns in the front of the

90

house, creating a beautiful tropical garden. Strains of exquisite harmonies and soft guitar music floated on the air. We were still at some distance from the others, and as yet I saw no sign of the guest of honor.

As we approached the house, I started to tell Jonathan about the first professor I had in philosophy. "He was a very interesting man who I admired greatly; he was one of those individuals who had a way about him that created great interest in the subject he was teaching. As a matter of fact, that same professor told me something very similar to what you once mentioned, that 'original' psychology was the study of the Spirit and Soul. He also told me that after fruitless study, the investigation of Soul and Spirit was dropped with the idea that they held no validity, and were irrelevant in the study of what is called psychology.

"In later years the same thing happened in study of consciousness. Again, it was too nebulous a subject and the study of consciousness came to an end."

"Interesting," Jonathan remarked.

I continued by explaining the next step in the evolution of psychology; the study of mind, and how through time this study became outdated, with the study of *behavior* taking its place.

We strolled to the house as Jonathan listened

intently to my explanation of the history of psychology. "Your professor might have been a lot smarter than you think. In fact, the way he described the original psychology is quite fascinating."

I wondered if there were teachers who understood the original psychology of Spirit, Soul, and Mind. Perhaps the things that Mamma Lila and Jonathan spoke of were closer to the true meaning of psychology than I had realized.

I could not help but think, "Just what kind of unbelievable storybook situation have I stumbled upon!" Never in all the years that I had lived in New York had I met two such incredible people as Mamma Lila and Jonathan; and believe me, I'd thought I had heard it all. Over and over again I kept asking myself, "Is it possible that two such ordinary, simple people have the answer that humanity and psychology have been searching for?"

For a moment, I was elated at such a profound thought, but then my brain dismissed the possibility. I couldn't help thinking that you don't just meet two perfect strangers who talk with such knowledge. After all, this is not Hollywood, *"this is real life!"* It was a strange feeling as part of me denied completely the mysterious chain of events that had happened on my previous visit to the

Hawaiian Islands. On the other hand, a deeper part of me *knew* somewhere that Mamma Lila and Jonathan had a direct link to the disappearance of my sickness. Apart from that I could not deny the dramatic, positive change in my outlook on life since first meeting Jonathan and Mamma Lila. I felt grateful to be with two such wise souls who were so willing to share their knowledge.

At the far end of the lawn we could see Mamma Lila seated in the shade. We strolled over to sit with her in the white wicker chairs facing the gardens. We spoke for a short while about the music and entertainment of the afternoon. Then, remembering my earlier conversation with Jonathan, I asked Mamma Lila, "Does the study of Soul and Spirit make sense to you?"

There was silence for a moment. "Of course! Soul is consciousness in motion, Spirit is the very breath of life!" she stated simply, while looking deep into my eyes.

She said it with such certainty that it stirred something within me. Her words aroused in me a feeling that she could answer more questions than any other person I had ever known.

I liked how she described Soul and Spirit, yet I still wanted to know where Mind fitted into it, so I asked her.

Her angelic face seemed to glow as she leaned her

head over and explained, "One cannot have consciousness without Mind. Mind is the SOURCE OF CONSCIOUSNESS. Consciousness indicates the presence of spiritual and physical realms."

With her reply she erased any further question from my mind and I fell speechless. Between the physical beauty around me and the conversation we were having, a feeling of overwhelming peace and tranquility filled my senses. My mind was clear and alert waiting for Mamma Lila to continue her intriguing philosophy.

But she ended by saying,

> "Treat your mind like your home;
> keep it clean and healthy.
> Do not harm anyone.
> Look for the positive side of life,
> keep your heart filled with Aloha
> and you won't go far astray."

We heard a song begin from the group of people near the house. One of them stood, then walked casually across the lawn toward us. He was a tall, powerful looking man with an infectious smile, as though he were laughing at a joke someone had just told. When he arrived he greeted both Jonathan and Mamma Lila with embraces and "Aloha's," then looked at me.

"Ah ha, someone I don't know yet! What a surprise." He winked at me as he bent over to shake my hand.

"I'm Toma, and you must be Richard."

Jonathan belatedly offered an introduction. "This is the infamous Toma, Lana's husband. I'm surprised you haven't met him yet. You'll always find him showing up when there's good music or good food being served."

"My job is to look out for quality control, and I take my work very seriously," he said with mock gravity, patting his belly. "It's my way of helping to preserve the Hawaiian heritage of good food." Jonathan chuckled in amusement. I remembered meeting Toma's wife Lana and their three children on my last visit to Maui. Her soft gentle manner had made an impression on me. As a couple they must be quite a pair.

Just then a little girl in a grass skirt and flower lei ran down the slope towards Mamma Lila. "Little Rosa, I can hardly believe it! You've grown into such a big girl! How old are you now?"

She raised four fingers to Mamma Lila. "Is that right... Well, let's see how good you can hug." A smile broke across Rosa's face and she rushed into Mamma Lila's arms. They embraced for a moment, this dignified old woman and sweet little girl. Then Rosa whispered something to Mamma Lila.

"It seems that the dancing will begin now; let's join the others."

We strolled up to the house where people were gathered, seated on woven mats and chairs arranged before the wide steps that rose to the veranda. As we approached, everyone fell silent, looking at Mamma Lila with respect. We seated ourselves in the front row next to the Makuas, where places had been kept for us. Toma mounted the steps and faced the small audience.

Extending his arms in a welcoming gesture, he called out a warm "Aloha" to everyone present. "Aloha" answered the voices all around us. Looking toward Mamma Lila, Toma spoke a few short phrases in the Hawaiian language. Many of the older people nodded and smiled at his words, Mamma Lila bowed her head slightly in response, gracing Toma with a broad smile of appreciation.

He went on, "Dear friends, it is now my pleasure to call out our keikis, our children, to share their Aloha with you." He backed up a few steps to where a guitar was waiting, picked it up, and began to play the rhythmical chords of a hula. A lovely middle aged lady wearing a mu'u mu'u and a large straw hat joined him on stage, vigorously strumming a tiny ukulele. From inside the house four beautiful little girls danced gracefully out onto the veranda. I recognized the youngest as little

96

Rosa. I was amazed at the grace of these children. Their green ti leaf skirts swayed in time to the music, their hands creating fluid gestures, all in almost perfect unison. Beautiful yellow and white plumeria flowers decorated their long dark hair and hung in garlands around their shoulders. The sweet smiles on their faces captured my heart.

The first lively hula was followed by a slower, very romantic song. Again I was struck by the loveliness of motion, and the beguiling expressions on the faces of the little dancers. Even Rosa, who had seemed so young and shy, had an unself-conscious grace on stage. Each hula was greeted by loud and long applause, whistles, and shouts of "Hana hou!" meaning "Encore!" and the little performers were happy to oblige. Several songs later, they concluded their show with a rousing number called "A 'o ia," which means "That's It!"

As the audience rose to a standing ovation, the dancers ran over to where we were seated and piled their leis around Mamma Lila's shoulders, showering her with kisses and "Aloha's." The crowd broke into groups of laughter and conversation, as a few more musicians joined Toma and the ukulele player in an impromptu Hawaiian jam session. Delicious scents wafted through the air, as an abundance of Hawaiian dishes were displayed on makeshift picnic tables.

In Quest of the Pearl

After some time had passed, I became aware that the music had stopped. Softly at first, then louder came the long, deep vowels of an ancient Hawaiian chant. Everyone grew silent to listen. Walking up through the audience was Toma, gesturing confidently, his whole body seeming to be moved along by the hypnotic sound of his voice - single notes, rising and falling in a subtly measured cadence, with quavering tones, and a strangely haunting quality. He walked up onto the veranda, knelt down on the floor, and picked up a gourd drum. He sat and struck the gourd in time to the rhythm of his chant, and the effect was mesmerizing.

The four little hula girls again appeared on the veranda, their flower leis replaced by wreaths of mountain ferns. Their movements to this drumming, while graceful, were different from before. There was a feeling in the air of ancient times, and I could picture the scene before me happening a thousand years ago.

The ancient hula ended, and the girls did a beautiful exit dance, facing the audience as their movements brought them back toward the door of the house. The chant continued, and changed into a song as the beating of the drum was accompanied by guitar and ukulele. Gliding out onto the stage as the young girls were going off, came the graceful

98

figure of Lana. She was wearing a long, Victorian style gown of deep pink, with sleeves of satin and lace, and a long ruffled train. On her head she wore a wreath of ferns and pink roses, and a long, open lei of rosebuds was intertwined with maile leaves around her shoulders. Her thick dark hair was swept up, and her face shone with a beautiful smile as her eyes followed the movements of her fingertips. She moved about effortlessly, her hips swaying gently, her hands softly telling a story of Aloha.

There was such a feeling of love being expressed as Lana danced, directed out to all of us, but especially toward Mamma Lila. I felt extremely fortunate to be sharing in such a beautiful experience, realizing I was witnessing more than the average tourist would ever see in a lifetime.

As the song ended, Lana's hands went to her heart and then out to Mamma Lila. In her sweet Hawaiian accent she said, "To you Mamma Lila, who have brought love into our hearts and wisdom to our lives. I cannot dream what life would have been like without you. Mahalo nui loa." Tears filled her eyes.

Everyone joined in hearty applause, and it seemed to be not only for Lana and the musicians, but most of all for the lady being honored. Rising gracefully, Mamma Lila beckoned Lana with her

arms. They embraced warmly as she said, "My little keiki is all grown up!"

Mamma Lila very quietly unfastened the gold bracelet on her wrist. "Lana, would you do me the great honor of accepting this bracelet?"

"Oh! Mamma Lila, I can't! It is so precious to you."

"My dear sweet one, that is precisely why I am giving it to you! Believe me, it would truly please me if you would accept it."

Mamma Lila then lifted Lana's hand and gently placed the bracelet around her wrist. Stepping forward, Lana embraced Mamma Lila again. "Mahalo nui loa, thank you from the bottom of my heart."

In all my life I had never realized that such pure love existed. The feelings that I felt were so strong and so beautiful that I could not contain my tears. There was no doubt that both Mamma Lila and Lana knew that something was nearing an end.

The afternoon flowed into evening, and we enjoyed a delicious feast of local foods, eating by the light of tiki torches beneath a starry sky. The whole day was one of the most beautiful times of my life, and a memory that is etched in my heart forever.

<u>Chapter</u>
<u>9</u>

A Walk in Iao Forest

The day before I was to leave Maui and return to New York, Jonathan called, inviting me to go with him for a walk in the forests of Iao Valley, which he told me was a very special place to the Hawaiian people.

"Iao Valley is steeped in history and legend," he explained, "and there is a unique feeling to the place - mystical and serene."

He went on to say that there were many trails

101

winding up through tropical forests, with a river running through the valley, and waterfalls cascading down sheer cliffs. "I hope you're in decent shape," he kidded.

We made arrangements to meet at my hotel, where he would pick me up for the drive across the island, to Iao State Park.

An hour later, we met in the lobby, and soon we were off, driving down the now familiar coastal highway, heading towards Wailuku and Iao Valley.

The scenery changed from dry scrub lands to lush rain forest as we reached the windward side of the island. We made the turn heading up towards the valley, and the vegetation became even thicker. I couldn't remember feeling so good in years. My whole body felt young and alive again, my mind sharp and clear. It was one of those days I will always cherish. I remember very little of what Jonathan said that day; on the contrary, it wasn't so much what he said, it was the incredible *feelings* I was experiencing that remain in my memory...

As we drove up the winding mountain road, I had a feeling of excitement and anticipation for the adventure we were beginning. It had been years since I had done any hiking, but Jonathan had assured me that the trails we would be travelling held beauty well worth the effort of the climb. We parked the car in the long paved lot of Iao State

Park, and climbed the hill of cement steps to the lookout point, where our walk through the forest would begin. As we paused to catch our breath and look around, I was overwhelmed by the beauty of the steep green mountains surrounding us. Soft mists floated above, partially obscuring many of the cliffs, but the Iao Needle stood out clearly against the sky. Jonathan had told me some of the history of this place, about the battle fought long ago by Maui's warriors defending their island against the forces of Kamehameha the Great, the king who eventually unified the Hawaiian Islands under his rule.

There was an energy here that could almost be seen, and I felt it intensify as we ducked beneath the iron railing and started up the trail. The smells and sights of the forest filled my senses and I was again delighted at the opportunity to explore this hidden part of Maui.

Eventually we broke away from the main trail, climbing over slippery boulders to arrive on a narrow, less travelled pathway. Jonathan was taking me to one of his favorite spots. There were no big trees here, only low ferns, deep green in color, growing in wild profusion. Our view all around was unobstructed, and it was breathtaking.

The trail was not easy, but somehow I didn't feel at all tired; it was as if I were being carried along by

103

the energy of the place. My mind was so filled with the beauty that there was no room for thoughts of anything else.

Eventually we came to a resting place, a little knoll with some rocks to sit on and a long view of the valley below. We could hear the thunder of waterfalls and see the river rushing between the steep valley walls.

As we sat, I felt a contentment and peace such as I hadn't experienced since childhood. The memory of sitting in church as a small boy came to me, the feeling of "all is well." I asked Jonathan, "What are your feelings about religion?"

"It depends on what you call religion."

He looked at me for a moment, then with a smile and a shake of his head he declared, "There are two things I rarely discuss... religion and politics. One of the reasons being, both religion and politics are very personal beliefs."

With that, Jonathan offered me a much needed drink of water from his canteen. We rose to continue our journey. Soon, the trail led us into a cool, shady grove of tropical forest. Touching one of many rose colored trees, I asked Jonathan what kind it was.

"They're guava trees," he answered, leaning over to touch the satin smooth bark of the branches, which twisted in graceful patterns. Calls of wild

104

jungle birds echoed through the trees, and I felt as if I were walking in a beautiful primeval forest, or a Hollywood movie.

At the next turn in the trail, Jonathan pointed out a small flowering tree growing just on the edge of a steep cliff. Its flowers were feathery and bright red. "This is the 'Ohi'a Lehua,'" he said. "The lehua flower is sacred to the Hawaiians, partly because it is so rare. Where you see lehua trees, you will often find the maile growing." Here, he gently lifted a strand of small, light green leaves which were growing on a vine, winding amidst the branches of the lehua tree. "The maile is another 'sacred plant.' It is used to make leis for very special occasions - weddings, graduations, and ceremonies of state. In the ancient days, its use was reserved for the 'Ali'i' - the Royalty, and priests."

The scents of the forest were sweet and pungent at the same time. I was experiencing a depth of feeling which was completely new to me.

We continued along the ridge pathway in silent fascination and contentment. As our trail took us on a gentle downward turn, I inhaled the fragrance of ripe guava, mixed with the rich scent of delicate white ginger blossoms, growing in abundance all around us.

It seemed we were travelling deeper and deeper into the forest. The air was cool, and patterns of

105

light and shadow danced around us.

We had seen very few people as we hiked, but now I could hear soft voices ahead. Soon we came upon a young couple walking toward us, and we exchanged greetings as they passed. The tenderness they exhibited toward each other shot a pang of jealousy through me. I felt a tightness in my chest as thoughts of my own dear wife raced through my mind. Why did she have to die so young? We had loved each other so much; I would have given anything to have her with me at that moment, to share in these new experiences with me.

I was lost in such thoughts for too long a time, when I became aware of the sounds of cascading water - faint at first, then louder as we continued our descent along the trail. I could feel a strange excitement building within. I felt drawn along the path as though I were walking in a dream. The feeling intensified as we approached the source of the sound.

Soon I knew we must be near; the sound filled the air around us. Jonathan pushed aside a veil of tangled foliage and a vision of mystical beauty appeared. Surrounded by lush vegetation was a crystal clear pool, fed by a small waterfall. To my utter astonishment, Mamma Lila sat silently at the water's edge. Her petite figure seemed to be

106

fashioned from the nature around her. Her face, as she gazed into the tumbling waterfall, was calm, almost like a child's. Her silver hair was swept back softly and braided into a bun. Her hands were folded lightly in her lap, and she wore a long, dark colored mu'u mu'u, its delicate floral pattern seeming to mirror the tiny flowers growing amidst the ferns around her. A beautiful maile lei was gracefully draped over her shoulders.

I couldn't take my eyes from this gentle soul, and I somehow wanted to memorize every detail of her expression. It pained me deeply to think that this might be the last time I would see her, and yet the power of her presence filled me with a feeling of peace more profound than I had ever known. I felt as if I could stand there and behold this scene for an eternity.

Breaking the silence, Jonathan walked up to Mamma Lila, greeting her with a hug and a warm Aloha. He didn't seem surprised to see her, but I was flabbergasted to say the least. Fondly embracing Mamma Lila, I expressed my delight at her presence. "It truly is a wonderful surprise to see you again." With a graceful gesture and a huge smile, she bade us sit with her by the water.

Lush green moss, overhanging the shimmering emerald pool provided a beautiful backdrop to the scene. The sound of the waterfall was like an

endless melody, punctuated by whistling calls of tropical birds. In a voice as musical as the forest, Mamma Lila entranced us with stories of Hawaii Past.

Sitting beside her, I could feel the radiance of her presence all about. I wanted so much to be at peace with this moment, but a persistent thought kept stealing into my mind, disturbing the tranquility, and bringing a tension to my body. Sensing my discomfort, Mamma Lila asked if I was worried about something. Her intuition never ceased to amaze me.

I started to explain how the loss of my wife was still so difficult to accept, and that what haunted me more than anything since her death was loneliness. The fact that I was only married six months made it even harder to understand why such a young woman should have to die.

Mamma Lila sat in silence and gazed towards the waterfall. Then turning, she said, "I understand how you feel."

Reaching over, she held both my hands and told me very straightforwardly, "Your wife, like my husband, came to her end because it was her fate, and fate is in the hands of one who is greater than we. Someday your wish might come true, and the understanding you seek will free you from such unhappy thoughts." Then, in a very soft voice she

108

explained how she had gone through similar feelings when her husband passed away.

"Were you married long?"

"Forty-five years," she said, "forty-five beautiful years we were together. We had a marriage that was like a precious wine, growing richer as time passed."

"It sounds like you were very much in love."

"We were, Richard. My husband was a gentle, loving man and a wonderful father to our children. He was a kind, wise person who lived each day in the state of Aloha. Then one day, he suffered a fatal heart attack, and in a few seconds our life together was over. At first, I was inconsolable, and my heart ached beyond anything I had ever experienced. My loss blinded me from using the power my kupuna kane (grandfather) had taught me, power that could change hate to love, and sadness to unparalleled joy."

"Then one evening I was watching the sunset, when, instead of the feeling of sadness, my heart filled with indescribable Aloha, and gratefulness at the thought of having shared forty-five years of my life with such a beautiful, loving person. My thoughts had turned to ones of gratitude instead of loss. I knew my wisdom and power had returned, setting me free from the torment I was going through."

In Quest of the Pearl

A feeling of humility washed over me as I realized the way I had been complaining about "poor me" since my wife had died. I looked over at Mamma Lila and felt the greatest respect for her. She was such a seemingly vulnerable person who must have gone through as much suffering as I, or even more! But her loss came without even one complaint. On the contrary, she expressed only love and gratitude. She struck me as being a very strong and wise person; there was an air of grace about her. There was something about her very presence that was different from most people.

She said, "You are a young man and have a long life ahead of you. I am sure some day soon you will find a beautiful wahine to share your world." Standing up, Mamma Lila lifted her arms toward the sky and said, "Throw your dreams and hopes to the heavens above. If you believe in them strongly enough, some day the Great One will sprinkle his Aloha over them and bring them to life for you."

At this point I was so touched by Mamma Lila's words I was speechless. Waves of incredibly beautiful feelings flowed through me, and my chest swelled as I fought back the tears. Deep in my heart her words lifted away a heavy burden, bringing an awareness that from this moment on, my life would never be the same. It was like a

great insight.   Jonathan had said all along "...simplicity, once your start to HEAR!"

I was overwhelmed by a deep sense of gratitude; grateful that my health had been restored, grateful that I had found such happiness, grateful to this gentle woman and Jonathan for all they had done to open my eyes. Before I could voice my thoughts she spoke again.

"Dear friend, I am so glad we have met. You have truly begun your journey home. Trust these Aloha feelings; they are your guide. They are the only clue you will need to lead you to the 'Pearl of Wisdom' that you seek."

With that, she turned her gaze to the scene before us. "When I was first married, my husband and I lived here on the island of Maui. Often we would come to this valley to share the peacefulness of the forest. I have known so much love and seen so much beauty here, yet soon I will leave this enchanting island forever. My home is calling to me and I must say farewell to my friends here."

We stood quietly for several moments, cherishing the feeling that we all shared. Then Jonathan stepped forward and embraced Mamma Lila. "Aloha, Mamma Lila, Aloha!"

They parted slowly, then I felt Mamma Lila's hand close about mine as she looked up into my eyes.

111

"God speed on your journey through life, young Richard."

Embracing Mamma Lila for the last time, my heart was so full I thought it was going to burst. After a pause, Jonathan suggested that it was time to head home.

He started walking toward the trail, and I followed reluctantly. Touching his arm I whispered, "We can't just leave Mamma Lila alone here in the forest."

Jonathan smiled and said softly, "Don't worry about Mamma Lila, Richard. Rest assured she will be well taken care of."

Only one week after I left Maui, Jonathan informed me that Mamma Lila had passed away in her sleep, both her children at her bedside. Jonathan, as far as I know, is wandering somewhere in this world; wherever he is roaming, my thoughts are often with him, and I wish him all the best.

As long as I live, I will never forget these two loving souls. Nearly two years have passed since that day we walked in Iao forest, and as Mamma Lila had predicted, I did meet and marry a beautiful wahine. My wife and I will be forever grateful for the Aloha and wisdom that Jonathan and Mamma Lila shared with me.

There is one more thing I would like to add, and

112

that is, if you are ever lucky enough to meet someone like Mamma Lila or Jonathan, listen to that person very carefully.

Listen with all your heart,
and someday, perhaps, you too
will come to find
dreams can come true.